P.F.GREGORY

The Ev
Among

First published in 2017

This Edition first published in 2017

Copyright © P.F. Gregory, 2017

All rights reserved. This book or any portion thereof may not be reproduced or used in any manner whatsoever without the express written permission of the author except for the use of brief quotations in a book review

P.F. Gregory asserts his moral right to be identified as the author of this book in accordance with Section 77 of the Copyright, Designs and Patents Act 1988

In this work of fiction, the characters, places and events are either the product of the author's imagination, or they are used entirely fictitiously. Any similarity to real persons, alive or dead, is coincidental and not intended by the author.

Cover design by P.F. Gregory. Cover image: Stock photo ID 213079843 Inked Pixels/Shutterstock.com, used under licence from Shutterstock.com

The Evil From Among You

P.F.GREGORY

Dedication

For my Aunty Lynda - a long time fan of a good whodunnit and one of the best advocates of my debut novel Kindly Invited To Murder.

Foreword by the Author

Having received positive feedback and reviews for my debut novel - and after many intervening months, my second whodunnit novel is complete and right here with you now.

For those of you who enjoyed following Davieson (and Kent for that matter) through the twists and turns of my debut novel *Kindly Invited To Murder*, I hope that I already have the forging of a consistent style and that you are thus soon back in familiar territory and able to once again escape from reality for a little while...but following the very latest sinister developments in an otherwise-respectable neighbourhood!
If you are new to Davieson, then welcome - and enjoy!

Thank you for letting me entertain you.

P.F. Gregory 21st August 2017.

Chapter One

It was mid-morning, on Thursday 4th July, and Ted Ellis stepped out on to the terrace, like *Nelson* onto the poop deck of *The Victory* at *Trafalgar*. Powerful field glasses hung around his neck. He set himself, and steadily brought them to his eyes to once more survey his dominion.

Panning slowly from left to right, across every inch of ground before him - and pausing every now and then to peruse and re-focus, Ted was assessing any items requiring attention from a distance, and gauging the day's work ahead.

Presently he removed the antique field glasses from his eyes in dismay:

'Moles!'

He let out a sigh:

'Little blighters. Still...nothing a shovel won't put right'

Upper Woodleigh Cricket Club had a home fixture at the weekend, and Ted was ensuring the wicket and outfield were ready and up to his usual high (and noted) standards.

The cricket club boasted a fine reputation throughout the *Haverton & District Cricket League* - and geographically well beyond this too, and this was largely down to Ted's lengthy and dedicated service to the club over the years.

Today's blot on the landscape would soon be rectified though. He'd carefully remove their earthworks for sure...*he may even gently tap one of them on the head with his shovel, should they surface whilst he was at it.*

The groundsman wheeled about and headed inside, into their pavilion-cum-clubhouse. Hearing their barman (Bob Butler) busily checking he was sufficiently stocked for the weekend's customers, he made for the storeroom (his storeroom) to collate the necessary tools and equipment and begin his own preparations.

He opened the storeroom door and made for his overalls hanging on a peg in the corner.

Suitably attired for a day outdoors, Ted Ellis sat down on his old and familiar wooden chair, looked around the storeroom and scratched his head in confusion. He tried to recall the previous fixture, tried to recall the last mow...but neither helped the source of his quandary.

He could still hear Bob rattling glassware from the direction of the lounge bar and thought the barman might help:

'Bob!' he yelled.

There was a suspension in the rattling activity, and presently Bob shouted back:

'Yeah?'

'You been in here this morning or recently??'

'No Ted'

'Do you know who might have been??'

'No sorry...maybe someone else on the committee??'

'Ok. I'm just wondering why they've had to move things around, that's all. I need to get cracking out there today, getting the ground in order - not wasting time ferreting around in here trying to find my tackle'

Bob Butler sniggered - well out of Ted's earshot. He quickly composed himself, put a tea towel down on the bar, and called back:

'Hang on Ted, I'll come down there'

The footsteps grew louder and in under a minute the club barman poked his head into the sanctuary of Ted's storeroom:

'Can I help?'

'Probably not sorry...but thanks anyway Bob. *Everything has its place* you know? You'd only make it worse...no offence'

'None taken Ted. None taken. Well, I'll leave you to it then, just let me know if I can help, all right? Anyway - is it a problem??'

'Just annoying really. I haven't found my *Wellington* boots yet...nor my gardening gloves for that matter'

'The trials and tribulations of a groundsman eh?' joked Bob.

Ted...already low on humour that day, gave him an unappreciative cold stare.

It was not lost on Bob and he tactfully disappeared, heading back towards the lounge bar and further pot washing.

A minute or two later and he was disturbed again, as Ted yelled once more from the other end of the clubhouse:

'You haven't seen my shovel have you, Bob?'

'No Ted!' yelled Bob Butler firmly - and with some finality.

The latter smiled to himself and shook his head...

***

The alarm clock rang the following morning, on the bedside table next to him - instantly awakening him from a deep deep sleep. He sat up in bed and groaned. He felt lousy. In fact, he hadn't ever felt as bad as *this* before.

There was a sleepy murmur next to him as his wife (disturbed by his alarm) rolled over and pulled the duvet tightly around her shoulder-tops.

He shook his head.

Andrew Knowles got out of bed and lethargically pulled some clothes on. He left the bedroom and trundled bleary-eyed - his body sticky from the alcohol-induced night sweats - across their landing and into the bathroom.

He pulled down the light cord, hastily wiped the sleep out of the corners of his eyes - and peered into the bathroom mirror.

I look dreadful! There's no way I can go into work looking like this! I must reek of booze in any case!

Andrew Knowles pottered downstairs, ran the cold tap for a good few seconds - and poured himself a large glass of nice cold water. He drank it straight down in one effort.

He looked at the kitchen clock. *Too early to do anything about it just yet.*

He sat down and knew he would shortly be doing something that he had never done before...Andrew Knowles would pull his first ever *sickie*.

He paced around his kitchen, contemplating the events that had transpired the evening before in the cricket club bar. The events would surely have played on his mind the night before, had he not drunk far too much that evening to remember anything. Now awake - it all came flooding back to him and occupied his mind.

Maybe not my cleverest move...but I just saw red!

Andrew Knowles put the kettle on, made himself a pot of tea - and waited until someone was bound to have opened the branch up.

Well here goes - the customer mortgage appointments would just have to be rearranged.

He picked up his phone and dialled.

A colleague answered.

'Hi - it's Andrew'

'Hi Andrew...you sound terrible - are you okay?'

'I'm afraid not - I think I must be coming down with something, so I won't make it in today. Can you look at my diary and rearrange the appointments for me, please?...Apologise re the short notice, if you wouldn't mind, too?'

'Of course Andrew...and I hope you feel better soon!'

'Thanks. I think that I'm going to get back in bed'
'You do that'
'Bye then'
'Bye Andrew'

He hung up just as his wife Deborah came down the stairs and into the kitchen. He had his back to her.

'Hi Honey...shouldn't you have left by now for the bank?'

He turned around and glared at his wife:

'You'd like me off out of the way wouldn't you?'

He put his shoes on hastily, let himself out of the front door - and slammed it shut behind him. The ferocity rattled the door frame.

Deborah Knowles ran to the door and opened it. Her husband was striding down the driveway and away from the house at some considerable pace.

'Where are you going?' she enquired nervously.

Andrew Knowles wheeled around and stared daggers at her:

'Just out!...'

***

Barely 7.30 a.m. and an expensive motor pulled onto the near-deserted seafront and parked up, engine still running.

Having satisfied himself that the spot was suitably conspicuous - and posed little danger to his beloved set of wheels, the man switched off the engine, stepped out - and locked his car.

He immediately walked to the railings at the side of the promenade, took in two good lungful's of sea air, and stared out to a calm sea. He smiled at the sound of a seagull screeching overhead.

Looking first up the lengthy prom, he set off and headed east, the sea and sky serene - his heartbeat racing...it always did at the start of the latest dalliance.

It was barely five minutes into this seaside stroll when he saw her - at the bandstand as promised. He paused in his tracks, his spine starting to tingle - and took a quick deep breath.

He moved off again...his steps now quickened, and in no time at all, they were upon each other and made eye contact.

'You came then?'

'I did' she replied smiling: 'I've no idea what I'm letting myself in for mind...but I'm intrigued'

He smiled back and put his hands upon her hips.

Neither spoke but they looked each other in the eye briefly and then kissed passionately.

She thought it felt the most natural thing in the world and was happy trusting her instincts.

He eventually drew away and looked her in the face, smiling:

'Well. First things first - a Knickerbocker Glory, or an ice cream?'

She laughed loudly and infectiously.

He laughed back.

'Oh ice cream every time...with a flake in it!'

'Of course, of course. Well, ice cream it is then'

He put his arm around her shoulder, pulled her in close - and together they headed off to find the nearest ice cream kiosk...

***

The kettle boiled and Craig Ellsmere poured himself a large mug of strong steaming coffee.

He took it through to his lounge, grabbed a packet of biscuits from the biscuit tin en route, and set them both down on a coffee table. He grabbed his A4 pad and a biro, and set himself to work.

Ten of the eleven would pick themselves of course, but what to do with the enforced change?

Craig Ellsmere was 1st XI Captain at *Upper Woodleigh Cricket Club* and responsible for team selection. He turned the options over in his mind:

He had to pick the other ten - they were in terrific form. On the plus side, he might not have his ear bent quite so much this game either. Yes - he would be firmly in charge of this one!

He reached for his mug - took a sip, burnt his lips, stroked his chin - and then absent-mindedly started to write *Roger*. He stopped himself before he got to the small *r*:

Would Roger do me a favour? Just this once??...No, of course not - perish the thought.

He'd thought of Roger before, but dismissed the idea then - and dismissed the idea now. He neatly ruled *Roger* out and continued to think.

Half a coffee later - and after a moment of enlightened (if unorthodox) inspiration, he'd made his bold decision:

It would be a big step up, as he was still very young - but he'd heard many a good word about him all summer. One-for-the-future they all said. Well, that's the answer to my prayers...it must be. He'd give him a chance - he'd bring the promising bowler in from their Youth Side for his First XI debut...

Chapter Two

It was four days later, on the Tuesday, when Geoffrey Wright pulled onto his drive, switched the car engine off - and sighed.

It had been a hellish day at the office, the forthcoming acquisition demanding long thankless hours - and the intensity and urgency proving both physically and mentally draining.

To cap it all, roadworks - and the resulting diversion, had additionally made it a frustrating drive home in an uncomfortably hot car. All in all, a horrible combination of hassle and trials, testing his fortitude and resolve to near breaking point.

He sat for a moment in the car to unwind, then decided he had best head inside as he needed to use the lavatory. A late coffee at the office, and the roadworks, hadn't helped!

Geoffrey Wright stepped out, locked the car and fumbled for his house keys in his trouser pocket. Having sought the brass key he was after, he turned the key in the lock, opened his front door - and first stooped to the ground to retrieve the day's post lying at his feet.

He quickly leafed through them, and found the pile included an attempted delivery notification:

We have been unable to deliver your parcel today. The item will be held at your local delivery office in Haverton and can be collected between the hours of 07:00-13:00 and 16:00-18:00...

He switched the house lights on, shut the front door - and locked it behind him. Quickly slipping off his shoes, he took the post through to his kitchen.

He opened and read the other letters - *nothing of interest*, then discarded their envelopes in his pedal bin. The notification he placed next to his car keys, lying where he always left them ready for the next time he would need his car.

He'd pick it up on the way into the office tomorrow morning.

***

A light breakfast - after a surprisingly good night's sleep, and Geoffrey Wright was driving into the town centre early the following morning.

It was Wednesday, and he was using *off-piste* back roads, that were still thankfully clear and moving - as not everyone had, as yet, cottoned on to this ploy, so he was soon parked up near the delivery office.

He got out of the car, and took the notification with him.

There was no queue in the delivery office, so he rang the buzzer and a lady promptly appeared to serve him. She took the notification he waved at her, checked the details thereon, and then disappeared briefly somewhere out the back, and out of sight.

She returned shortly, and handed him a small square parcel bound in packing tape, that had evidently proved too stout for his front door letterbox. He gave it a cursory glance (his name was printed on the top), said *thanks* - and returned to his car.

Placing it in his glovebox, he pulled off and continued to the office on further backroads, feeling suitably refreshed and ready for the day's business priorities. He was once again feeling motivated to playing his part in the complex affairs underway.

***

He'd survived the day, and so Geoffrey Wright made his way wearily back to his car.

He got in.

Seatbelt on, windows down - and he was soon driving once more through little-used backstreets. He was utilising his local knowledge to its fullest extent, to circumnavigate *Haverton* town centre and stay well clear of the roadworks.

It was already closer to the *forthcoming* weekend, than it was to the one just gone - and in an intense week, that felt great.

He put some classical music on, hummed along as best he could and drummed his fingers lightly on the steering wheel. All in all, he thoroughly enjoyed the drive home through the leafy suburbs.

What a difference a day could make!

Arriving home, the overworked businessman parked up, and was nearly out of his car when he remembered the parcel he'd collected earlier. He leaned across to the glovebox, opened it - and grabbed the parcel.

Entering the house, Geoffrey Wright gazed down but there was no post this evening. He slipped his shoes off, dumped his briefcase in the hall (he was done with it until the following morning) and headed for the kitchen.

Taking a bottle of *Sauvignon Blanc* out of the fridge, he poured himself a generous glass of wine and selected a sharp knife from his cutlery drawer.

He took a large quaff, sat down on a chair at his kitchen table, and carefully cut into the parcel through the packaging tape.

In no time at all the tape was removed and he opened the box lid.

He peered in, dropped the knife to the floor with a clatter - and raced to the downstairs lavatory where he was violently sick.

A feeling of deep revulsion swept over him and perspiration stood in large drops on his forehead.

Cleaning himself up - and regaining some kind of composure, he crept cautiously back to the kitchen door. He approached the table, duly arrived back at it - and braved looking down once more...still struck with horror at the dreadful and afflicting sight before him.

It was an eye...a horrible bloodied eye...

Chapter Three

A weary Geoffrey Wright was shaking that Thursday morning, as he carried both briefcase and parcel out to his car.

He unlocked it, put the two items on the passenger seat - and collapsed heavily into the driver's seat.

He had barely slept a wink overnight - mulling over and over in his mind about what to do. His choices, he determined, were somewhat limited.

Although physically hungry, he was so knotted-up that he had not been able to stomach his cornflakes either. They remained on the kitchen table, where he had attempted breakfast, next to an abandoned cup of coffee.

Nevertheless, his decision was made. *He wouldn't be frightened off by this unwelcome delivery...he would dump it and pretend that it had never happened.*

'Well here goes' he whispered to himself, and set off.

He chose an even quieter way into his workplace. Quieter roads - quieter hour. It was much much earlier than he would ordinarily have headed into the office, but he needed the roads to himself.

He had a secluded bridge in mind on the road out to *Blayton*.

As he neared the bridge, he started to decelerate and nervously wound his window down to its fullest extent. He checked his rearview mirror once more (he'd been checking it ever since he left the house), veered across the road, in the absence of any oncoming traffic - and gently mounted the kerb.

He inched the car till it was almost scraping the drystone walling, and hurled the package out of the window, and off the bridge...

***

The enraged cyclist slammed his brakes on and cursed:

'Bloody fly-tipper!'

The bike came to an abrupt stop and skidded slightly on the grassy path.

The discarded rubbish had come flying down from the direction of the bridge (giving him a start) and had landed on the towpath just in front of him, as he rode home from his night-shift, along his regular canal-side commute.

Ever the environmentally-conscious sort, the cyclist could not abide litter on the highway or in the countryside. He'd report this to the borough council for sure...and as was always the case, he saw red!

He promptly ditched his bike and scampered up the footpath steps that linked the road above with the canal towpath down below, to give the culprit a *piece of his mind*. A car revved its engine somewhere overhead.

Out of breath, he had just got to the roadside, when the maroon four-wheel drive vehicle disappeared round a bend at speed, and out of sight.

'He's in a hurry!'

He trudged back down to the towpath, irate...but secure in the knowledge that he could at least partially describe the miscreant to the authorities. He'd reported fly-tippers in the past (doing his bit as a good citizen) - and here he'd partially witnessed the offence.

The cyclist neared his bike, and only then decided to see why the driver had felt the need to tear away in such a hurry. *Probably disposing of electricals, batteries - or something else you're not allowed to put in your household bin.*

He bent down and picked the package up.

It wasn't sealed - and so he opened it...

***

Geoffrey Wright parked in his allotted spot.

A bold *RESERVED* sign kept the unworthy at bay, and generally proved an effective deterrent against the unauthorised use of his dedicated parking space.

He grabbed his briefcase and got out of the car.

Car park traversed - he strolled into the offices of *Latchfords & Co.* in a world of his own...and with a weight lifted off his shoulders. *The relief was fantastic!*

Blanking the receptionist who had attempted eye contact, he headed straight for his office, almost colliding with a colleague in the corridor upstairs.

'Morning Geoff...you okay??'

He turned:

'Okay??...yes. Yes - I'm fine thanks'

He entered his office, shut the door behind him and slumped in his chair.

***

He'd abandoned his commute home (given the circumstances), carefully stashing the package in his slimline cycling rucksack - and wheeled the bike around.

He remounted and tore off along the towpath, back in the direction from which he had just come, scattering startled ducks, Canada Geese - and a predatory heron in his wake. He was heading for *Police Headquarters*.

Full of adrenaline, his pace was now somewhat exceeding that at which he had been cycling home. He thought of the great lurking building he was headed for as he rode along, oblivious of the passing scenery.

He'd ridden past the place many a time, but never had a cause to go in. He wondered what the experience would be like.

In what seemed like no time at all he was there.

'Well here goes' he said to himself.

He chained his bike to a cycle rack, took the rucksack off his back - and entered the building. He found a duty sergeant at the front desk:

'Good day sir'

'I errr...found this!'

He sat the package down on the desk top between the two of them.

The duty sergeant withdrew his hands away from the item, and promptly folded them. He eyed the cyclist cautiously:

'And what might that be sir?'

'It's an...errr, eye!'

'*An eye??*'

'That's right'

The duty sergeant stared down at the package, and then back at the cyclist. His arms remained tightly folded:

'You sure about that sir??'

'I'm sure. I wouldn't joke about that sort of thing, I assure you!!'

'Calm down sir. We have to careful nowadays, that's all. Some folk with queer ideas think it's a good idea to send *the boys in blue* letter bombs and suspicious packages from time to time'

'Well not this one'

'Errr no. Well...you better take a seat in the waiting room'

The duty sergeant pointed, and the cyclist headed off in the direction indicated.

He was kept waiting around ten minutes, wiling away the time by perusing the *Crimestoppers* literature dotted around the waiting room. He was sweating profusely after his extended morning's cycle ride.

He was just reading about the prevention of cycle theft, when a head popped around the door:

'Follow me please sir'

He was led into an interview room where they read him his rights (*a formality they assured him*) and advised him that he needed to make a statement.

He readily consented.

'Right then sir. Where did you find this parcel please?'

'On the canal towpath leading out of *Haverton*'

'It's a lengthy canal, sir - can you be more precise please?'

'Of course, yes...sorry'

He described the bridge he had been approaching earlier, when the package had come sailing through the air in front of him from overhead.

'And it was just lying there on the towpath was it??'

'Errr, no. Someone had chucked it off the bridge'

'*Chucked it off the bridge*?? Did you see who sir?'

'No...but I know the type of car they were in'

'So you saw *someone* throw this parcel out of their car'

'Well not exactly, no'

'*Not exactly*??'

The cyclist thought he had been acting responsibly in dashing immediately to *Police Headquarters* with his find, and had done the right thing. The experience (however), was not proceeding exactly how he had envisaged it might - and he was regretting having bothered in the first place.

'The package landed near my bike you see. I raced up to the road and saw a car speeding away'

'You raced up *on foot*??'

'That's right, yes'

'I see'

The policeman made a series of notes, read them through to himself - and then looked back up at the cyclist:

'So you found an eye. You dismounted your bike. You left your bike. You got yourself up onto the road level from the canal towpath beneath...and you saw a car pass? Is that correct sir?'

'Well, I guess so. Yes'

'I see. This car then - describe that please'

'It was a four-wheel drive vehicle'

'And did you make a note of the registration'

'I didn't I'm afraid. It was too far away, and travelling too fast for me to take a note of it'

A look of both disappointment and frustration grew ever larger on the policeman's face.

'Nevermind. Did you recognise the model sir??'

'Errr no...sorry'

'Colour??'

'Colour, yes. It was maroon'

The cyclist smiled at the policeman - feeling useful at last.

The friendliness was not returned:

'Well that's something at least'

The policeman completed his notes - read them through to himself, and after a couple of minutes or so looked up:

'Well there's just one final thing for now...we'll need to take your fingerprints sir'

'*My fingerprints*??'

'That's right sir - this way please...'

Chapter Four

'Much happening in the showbusiness department??'

'Quiet week Merv, but I'm still hopeful - there's a terrific new play opening in the *West End* tomorrow night, so I'll be going along to that. The word is there should be a fair few celebrities in attendance! Crime??'

'Nothing newsworthy I'm afraid. Still - a chance to get my expense claim in at least'

His colleague laughed, and then the two men finished their cigarettes and left the designated smoking area, to head their separate ways within the headquarters of *The Morning Chronicle.*

Merv Davieson (Davieson, to those who knew him) was Chief Crime Reporter at the reputable daily, and chose rare quieter moments to catch up on admin. The six foot tall Welshman, with sandy-coloured hair, trudged back up the flight of stairs to his office.

He smiled when he saw that a fellow reporter had kindly made him a fresh mug of coffee. *Maybe they could tell he was bored?*

He slumped down in his chair, let out a sigh of resignation - and opened his drawer to retrieve the, part-started, outstanding and overdue expense claim form that he had been slowly but steadily completing for far too many days now, constantly deprioritising its completion behind anything Davieson could argue was more pressing. He didn't struggle for applicable subject matter!

He grabbed his wallet from his light grey sports blazer, hung over his chair, opened it and removed a fistful of receipts.

Following the developments of a juicy story...particularly a case that ran and ran, could be an expensive business. There was sustenance for himself, relentless fuel costs, coffees and beers with members of the public willing to give his newspaper a comment or opinion - the expenses went on and on...

Fortunately, he wrote unrivalled quality articles - popular with his editor...and popular with the loyal readership.

No, Davieson, had never had a problem being *funded* to date - but red tape had necessarily increased over the years, and everything now had to be ship-shape and transparent for the newspaper's finance department, and their independent auditors.

He was just reminding himself of a receipt particulars when his phone rang. He didn't think twice about putting the receipt straight down on his desk. He lifted the receiver:

'Davieson??'

'That's right'

'It's Kent'

Davieson smiled. Under any professional circumstances, this unexpected call was most welcome:

'Chief Inspector! How are you?'

'Well, thanks, Davieson. The reason for the call is that we've something macabre afoot that might be right up your street'

Davieson had helped Scotland Yard on a murder case that had attracted sustained national interest - *The Bathcombe Bay Mystery*, and Kent's own men on a complex affair surrounding a wedding. He was the tall detective's favourite (and most trusted) journalist, and Kent found the amiable Welshman's fidelity second to none.

'I'm intrigued Chief Inspector...go on'

'A member of the public dropped into our place and deposited an eye with us!'

'*An eye*??'

'That's right. Not his own I might add - but one that had been packaged up in a small parcel'

'For posting??'

'It had been posted we believe. It looks like a (now-removed) postal address would have been taped to the top of it - but there's no addressee now, and no postal or franking marks'

'I see. And it's human??...the eyeball I mean!'

'It's human alright'

'Lovely! Are you thinking some *Jack the Ripper* lunatic??'

Kent ignored the sarcastic humour and kept it factual:

'Not *Jack the Ripper*, no. Our Police Surgeon is adamant that this eye definitely *hasn't* been surgically removed. More like a screwdriver he thinks...the eye was rather bloodied, and badly damaged at the back. The eye-socket itself *structurally compromised!*'

'You mean butchered I guess, Chief Inspector?'

'Well I guess so, yes' conceded Kent: 'I was quoting the surgeon direct'

'Butchered it is then -I like a description suited to the language of the press'

Kent gave the briefest of polite smiles that was unseen and undetected by the listening Welshman.

Davieson nodded thoughtfully. There was a short pause and he fired off another question:

'Anyone in the frame as yet?'

'Well it wouldn't be the first time a perpetrator led us to the *scene of a crime* so to speak, so we haven't ruled out the cyclist who brought the item in as yet. He *says* he saw a car driving away from (or past) the area, but no one else has come forward as yet, to say that they saw similar, so we only have his word for it'

'And this *scene of the crime??*'

Kent detailed the canal bridge in question.

'Can I meet you there Chief Inspector?'

'Of course Davieson. It'd be great to catch up anyway, and I can pick your brains at the same time. You'll see our police cordon and an officer on duty'

'I'm on my way...'

***

Davieson parked up, walked up to the cordon - and addressed the constable guarding the footpath that led down from the bridge to the canal towpath:

'Hello. I'm here to see Chief Inspector Kent'

'Name??'

He flashed his press pass in the constable's face:

'Davieson. I'm from *The Morning Chronicle*'

The constable checked the details and photograph on the pass, then studied his face briefly to assure himself that the gentleman had both the right credentials...and was who he said he was. He was happy the sandy-coloured haired man in front of him, with light blue eyes - and wearing oval-shaped spectacles, was *Mervyn Davieson*:

'This way sir'

Davieson followed the constable, and found Kent deep in thought on the canal towpath. A colleague of his was on his hands and knees, and busy studying what looked like bicycle-tyre skid marks in the dirt.

The journalist offered his hand:

'Chief Inspector'

'Davieson!...that'll be all thanks constable'

The constable nodded his head to his superior officer, repeated the gesture to Davieson - and returned to his posting. Kent relaxed his firm handshake and released Davieson's hand.

'So...plenty keeping your boys busy??'

'Well nothing as exciting as that wedding affair to be frank...until this little matter here of course'

'And this is where the cyclist says he saw the parcel land, and then brought it into you??'

'So he says yes. Certainly looks like he brought his bicycle to an abrupt halt here for some reason'

'Do you believe him?'

'I'm not sure Davieson. There's this car he says he saw driving away...'

'Ah yes, the car Chief Inspector. Any more to go on there?'

'Well the cyclist says that it was travelling at speed, but, from his fleeting glance, believes that it was a maroon four-wheel drive vehicle'

'Well, there can't be *thousands* of those on the roads I guess??'

'No, that's right. We're making enquiries and drawing up a possible list of further enquiry'

'And the car was travelling??'

'Says he scrambled up the footpath you just descended, as the car sped off in that direction'

Davieson's eyes followed Kent's hand gesture:

'That would be heading towards....*Blayton*??'

'That's right'

'So Blayton residents, owning a maroon four-wheel drive vehicle, may be the focus of your immediate enquiry??'

'They may be, yes'

The Welshman nodded thoughtfully, and remained silent for a moment or two. He took out his notepad and penned a few notes:

'And the direction the cyclist was headed??'

Kent pointed down the towpath, and under the road bridge:

'That way. He was heading home (he says) from a night shift in *Haverton*'

'And any fingerprints on the package?'

'Only the cyclist's! Says he always cycles in fingerless cycling gloves in the summer. If the parcel wasn't his - then whoever handled it before him, wore gloves'

'And what significance do you attach to the eyeball Chief Inspector?'

The tall policeman shook his head, flexed his right leg - and seemed to kick an imaginary football into the canal:

'I don't know Davieson. Did somebody see something they shouldn't have? Did someone look at something they shouldn't have?...was somebody spying on someone, had their cover blown...and the spied-on take offence??'

Kent shrugged his shoulders. Davieson stopped scribbling:

'...So you're looking for some sort of *curtain twitcher* maybe?...'

Chapter Five

Friday morning and there was an authoritative knock at his front door. He checked the time on the kitchen clock mounted on the wall, put the spoon back in his bowl of cornflakes - and trudged to the door in carpet slippers.

He found two police officers on his doorstep.

'Sorry to disturb you at this early hour, sir. Is it Geoffrey Wright??'

'Errr, yes - that's me'

'And is that your car parked on the driveway sir?'

They indicated behind them, and he glanced at his vehicle over their shoulders, still parked where he had left it the following evening. He held his composure...and nodded to the affirmative:

'It is, yes'

'Anyone else at home sir?'

'No - just me...I live alone'

'I see. So only you would use the car?...is that right sir??'

'That's right, yes'

'And can you tell me where you've driven it in the last twenty-four to forty-eight hours please sir?'

'*Twenty-four*??...what's this about please?'

'We'll ask the questions, for now, please sir'

'Sure...I'm sorry'

'Where exactly then please sir??'

'Just to and from work...nowhere else'

'And where is work, sir?'

'*Haverton*'

'It's a large town. Can you be more specific please sir?'

'*Latchford & Co.*'

'And your occupation sir?'

'I'm the Chief Accountant...the firm's *numbers* man!'

'And what route do you take into *Latchfords* sir?

'Well I drive straight there on the *Haverton Road*, and then normally continue straight along *Main Street* to the office...but when I hit the outskirts this week, I've been skirting around the suburbs instead...to avoid the roadworks. A slightly longer journey - but I'm finding it quicker'

'I see sir. And have your routes taken you out *Blayton* way at all in this timeframe?'

'*Blayton*?? No, it's out of my way, work is busy and time precious I'm afraid...*time is money* I should say in my position'

He laughed but there was no hint of a smile on the officers' faces, and an awkward silence followed.

One of the officers finished writing the notes he was making and broke the silence:

'And what's the best contact number that we can reach you on sir, if we have any further questions?'

He gave them the details.

'Well, that's all for now sir. Good day'

He watched them walk down the drive, and return to the patrol car parked on the road outside his house. He wondered if the neighbours had noticed it...*some of them were bound to have.*

He shut the door and his steely resolve immediately crumbled.

Surely no one had seen him dump the package??

Geoffrey Wright returned to the kitchen shaking, picked the bowl of cereal up, studied it for no more than two seconds - and emptied the contents straight into his pedal bin.

He had well and truly lost his appetite...

***

In the offices of *The Morning Chronicle*, Davieson was working on a new story - and one that he felt had mileage in it. *This one could run for a good few days yet, he was sure of it.*

His eyes twinkled and colleagues thankfully left him to it - they could tell when the Welshman was *in the zone*, and entranced with his work. He was largely unaware of their presence and in full flow!

The story would not yet be published (*Kent had asked him to hold fire for now*), but the tall policeman had assured him that he could publish his exclusive as soon as he gave him the all-clear.

Davieson was comfortable with this - he had honed a professional relationship with the Chief Inspector, built on solid foundations of trust. Any abuse of that, and it would be both the end of exclusives such as this one - and the end of one his key sources of information when trying to fill column inches for his employers.

He took a sip of his piping hot coffee, looked at the photograph he had taken at the canal towpath, and started to kick possible working titles for his article around in his head.

Mutilation by Mail??

He shook his head and instead concentrated on firming up the story itself.

***

She found the place quite easily and drove up the lengthy drive, giggling at the thought of surprising him like this!

Lovely digs!

Turning up unannounced and out of the blue - with a chilled bottle of Prosecco in hand, to say thank you for a fabulous long weekend at the coast. *He'd be surprised alright...but in a good way.*

The leggy dark-haired girl topped up her lipstick, got out of her car - and walked excitedly and elegantly up to the front door. She thought he might stay on after tomorrow's game, and want a drink with his cricketing pals...but *Friday night* should be up for grabs - and what a great way to start another weekend!

In the car, she left sufficient essentials that she had pulled together earlier, should an overnight stay be on the cards. *She'd leave them there for now, and see how the evening developed. Best not to presume too much...but be prepared just in case!*

She took a deep breath and rang the doorbell, unable to wipe the widest of smiles off her face. She felt like a teenager again and couldn't wait to pick up where they had left off at the weekend.

She gave it a while, but there was no answer.

She tried again...but still no joy.

She looked around and tried a shout. *Was he in his garden?? No, unlikely - there was no sign of the expensive (and quite lovely) car that she had also taken a fancy to either.*

His driveway was empty, and for whatever reason, he wasn't at home.

She took the bottle dejectedly back to her car, got in - and drove off.

The lady in the car parked up, in view of the house (but discreetly at a distance from it) looked confused. She stared open-mouthed through her windscreen for a while then shook her head. *Not what she had expected when she had decided to drive over on a whim earlier that evening, to try and evidence things for herself.*

She waited until the girl had driven safely off, and then started her own car engine.

She shook her head again before engaging first gear and pulling off:

Still, I'm not surprised with him...I've known him too long for that after all - and suspected as much for some time!

She drove back to her parents to further think things over again...

***

Andrew Knowles tore along *Rowley Hill Lane*. He was agitated, he was maniacal...he was angry!

They'd pulled the pair of them apart - he probably thought that was the end of it, but no...it wasn't over yet. His pride had been wounded - he had to finish this once and for all!

He wondered what he would have to say for himself?

He himself??...he'd let his fists do the talking!

Alone in his thoughts...and driving erratically, he almost clipped wing mirrors with a lady who had just pulled off from a parking space.

It pulled him to his senses...for three seconds at best, so he parked up in the space that the other driver had just vacated. He stepped out, slammed the car door shut, locked up - and marched off to confront his foe.

The man in black - who had been keeping himself to himself, had just managed to leap off the road and onto the grassy verge as Andrew Knowles screamed past.

It had been an instinctive (and necessary) last minute course of action...else he would have surely been run down! The absence of any high vis clothing about his person, could not have given the driver any warning that he was walking in the road - but he had no need to be driving at those speeds anyway.

He was just thankful he was still alive...he had no idea how the two cars had missed each other though!

Suitably shook up, he was now not in the right frame of mind - and in no fit state, to see through his planned tête-à-tête. *It would have to wait...for now!*

He turned around and instead started to walk home...

Chapter Six

It was Monday the 15th July. The start of a new week, and in his office at *Police Headquarters*, Kent was quietly reading through the various testimonies of the maroon four-wheel drive vehicle owners, that they had so far managed to locate and speak with.

There was only a handful of them to read through - maroon evidently not the most popular car colour of choice.

The testimonies were *much of a muchness*, all full of denial (possible evasion) and fairly minimalist in detail. Kent shook his head and tutted to himself. *Had his men asked the right questions??*

He suspected not.

He mulled things over for a while, and then thought once more about whether the package had been posted or not. They suspected it had, and maybe postal records could narrow the search down further.

If the person who discarded this believed they hadn't been observed - and who would have thought a cyclist might be passing at that hour for that matter?...then would they simply have binned the postage label??

They might do.

He wrote down *search rubbish bins* on a notepad in front of him, and rose in order to set his men upon the task immediately.

***

He was once again heading out of *Lower Woodleigh*, and climbing up *Rowley Hill Lane*, heading towards the local beauty-spot.

He drove his car steadily along the hedgerow-lined lanes, snaking this way and that through the lovely open countryside. As he saw the large barn conversion - set back from the road in lovely grounds, he turned off left onto a smaller lane skirting mature woodland.

Just past the long drive up to the property, there was a compacted-earth lay-by at the eastern entrance to *Rowley Woods,* and the man pulled onto it.

It was the lay-by regularly used by dog walkers and ramblers alike, who either lived some distance away from the pretty woodland…or were local, but preferred to keep the duration of their walks as short as physically possible.

An already excitable dog sat on the back seat, and recognised this was the start of *walkies!*

He switched the engine off, stepped out of the car and folded back the driver's seat. Holding the driver's door wide open he gave the usual command:

'Walkies'

Within a second, the dog leapt out of the back seat, hurtling through the air till he landed gracefully at his master's feet. Panting hard, he looked expectantly (and obediently) up at his owner, *chomping at the bit* for the always-welcome second command.

The man first reached over to the passenger seat, grabbed the little-used retractable dog leash and locked his car:

'Go on boy'

The dog raced off and entered the woodland by the footpath feeding off the lay-by. His owner - as he always did, followed him in his own time.

It was a beautiful sunny morning, dry underfoot - and birdsong filled the air. A perfect day for his favourite walk with the dog, and whilst the latter busily entertained himself exploring the undergrowth, and sniffing around his favoured patch - the man enjoyed the solitude, and a chance to clear his head.

Several paths criss-crossed the woods, and a well-crafted combination of these made for an interesting and delightful circular walk, comfortably achieved within the hour.

He whistled softly and little broke the tranquillity - save birdsong (mainly woodpigeons) and the occasional twig snapping under his boot, until he heard the clock on *St. Catherine's* strike 8 a.m.

Around halfway through his walk - at the western end of the woods, he stepped slightly off the well-trodden path and caught the usual glimpse of *Upper Woodleigh's* cricket ground, resplendent in the sunshine.

He paused for a moment or two to admire the immaculate wicket - starkly contrasting with the wild and dense undergrowth he was currently stood in. A myriad of grasses, ferns, nettles and brambles thrived three feet deep in places, and he was glad he resisted the temptation earlier, to pull on a pair of shorts.

He hadn't seen the dog as yet, but there was nothing unusual in that. The dog knew his way around well enough, and the woods were his playground - *let him enjoy it and work himself up an appetite.*

He returned to the path - which now headed north in the direction of *Rowley Hill Lane*, not a soul (man nor beast) in sight.

When he once again neared the lay-by - and having now completed his woodland walk in its entirety, without the company of his dog *(so much for man's best friend)* he decided to call him in:

'Toby'

He waited a minute...nothing.

'Toby!'

Further time for the dog to get his bearings...but still nothing. He shook his head in frustration and confusion, cleared his throat with a preparatory cough, and (cupping his hands around his mouth to make a funnel) yelled once more:

'TOBY!!!'

He stood perfectly still and stifled his breathing, straining his ears for any clue as to Toby's whereabouts.

Suddenly he heard a rustling in the undergrowth, then bounding footsteps getting louder by the second.

Toby bolted out from a clump of ferns and up to his master.

He breathed a sigh of relief:

'There you are, I thought I'd lost you!'

He patted Toby's head gently.

Toby barked, looked up at his master - and promptly shot off again in the direction of whence he came.

'What now' exclaimed his owner, and started to jog in the same direction:

'TOBY - COME HERE!'

He fought his way through the bracken and brambles, Toby frequently running part way back to him, to assure himself that his master was still following the trail.

Eventually, Toby stopped in a small clearing (to the breathless man's relief) and sat himself dutifully at a pile of loose earth. Broken fronds of bracken littered the area.

The man now noticed that Toby's nose and paws were all muddied and covered in earth:

'Well, you'll need a bath when we get you home I'm afraid! Anyway, what have you found - a rabbit??'

Toby just sat there panting and looked up at his master.

The man walked over to the mound of earth, curious to see what had detained Toby for so long that morning.

And then he saw it.

...Well, the grey hair at least.

He shuddered:

'Yuck...'

***

The wind in the hair was exhilarating...particularly on the many downhill sections, and when a breeze occasionally got up.

Yes - you never forget how to ride a bike, and you never lose that sense of freedom and independence when doing so.

The blue car parked outside the village post office had a parking ticket affixed to its front windscreen, held in place under the car's window wiper blades.

The cyclist rode just past it and mounted the kerb. Having rested the bike carefully outside the post office window display, the cyclist peered inside, through the glass, and patiently waited for a customer to leave.

It was one of those typical village post offices, dotted throughout the country, that doubled-up as both the village newsagents and the local convenience store. It was jam-packed full of produce, stationery, gift cards and newspapers.

Not the young girl who served me last time, today - the postmaster himself by the looks of it.

The cyclist waited until the previous customer had left and walked some distance away, entered the post office - and headed for the counter. The postmaster finished some paperwork and looked up smiling:

'Morning'

'Morning. I'd like to post this please'

The cyclist handed a small package to the postmaster.

The postmaster pointed at a clock on the wall:

'The postman has collected already today (I'm shutting up soon). It will go tomorrow now - is that ok??'

'That's fine yes...no problem'

'Right - signed for? Special Delivery? Standard Delivery?'

'Standard Delivery is fine thanks'

'Righto'

The cyclist paid the postage and returned to the bike.

When the post office was again empty, the postmaster stepped out from behind the counter, and walked over to the window display, with a poster advertising the forthcoming village *Open Gardens* weekend, and a clump of *Blu-Tack* in his hands.

He affixed the poster to the inside of the window, and saw the cyclist mount the bicycle on the pavement outside.

The cyclist whistled casually, and promptly rode away...

***

The receptionist on the front desk at *Haverton Borough Council* sat filing her nails - it had been a slow and quiet morning at the *Council Offices*, and resenting her relatively low wage, she was taking the opportunity to pamper and groom herself at her employer's expense...or the taxpayers' at least!

Having finished filing (fingernails not paperwork that morning), she put the emery board back in the handbag that was stashed safely out of sight, under the desk.

The reception was still empty, so she decided that there would be no harm done in leaving the desk unmanned for a while, and went to make herself a coffee at the small kitchenette down the corridor.

She found the kettle was already hot from a colleague's recent visit, so she was not away from the desk for any real length of time at all. Nevertheless, as she carried the hot coffee carefully back to reception, she found a man there just about to ring the *ring for attention* buzzer.

She headed him off and caught his eye:

'Good morning sir. Can I help?'

'Hello...I believe so. Yes, I'd like to report a dead animal'

'Ooh...dog is it?'

She screwed her face up, visualising the aftermath of a messy road accident.

The man nodded:

'That's right yes'

The receptionist reached for a form and took the top off her pen:

'Right, let me take down some details, please. Have you ran over the dog, sir?'

'*Have I??*...no, no I haven't killed it'

'And did you see who did kill the dog, sir?'

'I didn't I'm afraid. Sorry'

'No problem sir. And what road did you find the dog on please?'

*'Road??...*I'm sorry - I should have said. It's not on the road. No - somebody has dumped a dead dog in *Rowley Woods*'

The receptionist wrote down *Rowley Woods*, then looked up from the form:

'And can you describe exactly where you found the dog, sir?'

The man seemed to consider the question for a moment, then shook his head:

'I can't I'm afraid - there are so many trees there you see...I could take your chaps to the spot though, to help them retrieve it'

'Let me take your full contact details down then please sir'

The man left his details...

Chapter Seven

The police had swiftly consulted the council refuse collection schedule, and prioritised their visits accordingly.

If there was any mileage in their superior's suggested line of further enquiry, they had to ensure potential evidence was readily available to sift through meticulously - and wasn't dissipated amongst hordes of other households' waste, throughout the large local landfill site. If they *missed the boat*, their efforts would be reduced to a pitifully ineffective one, something along the lines of *a needle-in-a-haystack* exercise.

Next on their rounds was Geoffrey Wright.

They returned to his property, parked up on the street outside - and stepped out of the vehicle.

One of them rapped the door.

They gave it a good half a minute, and then rapped again...there was still no answer.

'Not back from *Latchfords*??'

'I guess not...we'll wait in the car'

The two police officers returned to the patrol car and awaited their subject.

Twenty minutes later, Geoffrey Wright drove down his street in his maroon four-by-four. He slowed (almost braking), astonished and dismayed at the presence of a police patrol car, once more parked at the end of his drive.

How long had they been there? The neighbours can't help but notice this time. Someone must have seen me throw the package off the bridge...

He gazed at the policemen, as he pulled on to his drive and parked up. His neighbour's curtains twitched, and he caught a brief glimpse of his elderly neighbour beating a hasty retreat back behind them.

His heart sank.

Brilliant!

He looked in the rear-view mirror, and saw that the police officers had stepped out of the patrol car and were striding up his drive.

'Well here goes...'

He got out of his own vehicle:

'Oh, hello'

'Sorry to trouble you again Mr. Wright, we're going to have to search your bins I'm afraid'

'My bins??'

'Yes - purely routine...I'm sure you understand'

Should he resist and challenge them??

He decided against it:

'Well if you must...but I really don't understand...'

'Don't worry yourself, sir - we'll take the contents job-lot, and won't need to detain you further this evening. Shall we start inside??'

He led them into the kitchen and pointed out the kitchen pedal bin. He then led them round the house and highlighted a further two wastepaper bins. Finally, they were taken outside to his wheelie bin.

The officers carefully bagged and labelled everything in tamper-evident carry bags (they had evidently come prepared!), reassured him once more - and made their departure, citing further pressing visits on their schedule.

He closed his front door behind him, grateful for the brief respite - the experience had been traumatic, and his nerves were fraught. *What must his neighbour be thinking??* He was quite glad to see the back of the police...*for now, he suspected.*

He headed for his kitchen, but stopped after a few short paces. He remembered the packaging label. He was sure now that he'd simply binned it. He wished he'd burnt it...

***

The next morning - Tuesday 16th July, and Toby could not understand why parking up at the lay-by, had not meant *walkies*. He whimpered periodically, and looked at his master sat in the front of the car, with despondent doleful eyes.

The council van eventually pulled onto the lay-by, a full thirteen minutes later than had been arranged, and two men in council uniform got out. They strolled over to the car:

'Sorry we're late sir - the roadworks are terrible in town'

'That's ok, I'm fine for time'

He folded his seat down and Toby jumped out wagging his tail furiously. His master remembered the lengthy abandonment on their previous visit, and decided it was wise to put his leash on this time.

'Well. Lead the way please sir'

'Right - follow me then'

He retraced the steps he had taken when he had followed Toby to his gruesome find, and in a few moments, he had successfully located the spot.

'Thank you, sir. We'll take it from here please'

'Ok...well I'll leave you to it. Good day'

He headed back to his car. Toby would not find today's walk one of his longest or most enjoyable...he hoped he wasn't too disappointed.

They returned to their car and headed back to *Lower Woodleigh*.

Back in the woods, the two councilmen had started to clear the earth from around the body, ready to retrieve the carcass and remove it from the woodland.

'It's a *Yorkshire Terrier* look. No mistaking that steel-grey and tan coat'

They continued to respectfully exhume the carcass, taking it in turns to spread the workload.

One of them promptly threw his shovel down and straightened his back:

'This dog hasn't died naturally Dave...someone's run it through with something sharp!'

'Accident, do you reckon?'

'Doesn't look like it'

Dave peered down and viewed the ghastly wounds visible along the dog's ribcage. He counted them, 1,2,3...

'It's been stabbed three times...stabbed deeply too!'

His colleague shook his head:

'There's some cruel folk around for sure. Can't understand how anyone could do that myself - can you??'

Dave shook his head:

'It's senseless'

'We should advise the *Animal Welfare* boys'

'Best inform the police too...'

***

The lay-by was utilised to its fullest capacity. Two patrol cars had parked up alongside the *Haverton Borough Council* van, leaving no room for anyone else to park safely or nearby. Dog-walkers and the like would have to find a new route today - and anyway, their presence would probably intrude on a necessary (but unpleasant) task at hand.

Dave had remained at the site of the exhumation, deep within the woodland - and his colleague had returned to the van to met the arriving police officers.

He led them through the thicket, to where Dave stood patiently, with his hands on his hips. A couple of dirtied shovels were propped up against an ancient oak.

Photographs were taken (key evidence they would need to bring a successful case of animal cruelty and neglect...if they could establish dog ownership) - and then a square cordon was established between four trees bordering the small clearing.

Dave stood there fascinated.

A policeman looked at him:

'We'll take it from here thanks, sir'

Dismissed, Dave headed back to his council van, a trifle disappointed. When safely out of earshot the policemen conversed:

'The wounds look fairly uniform alright - and deep too. Five or more inches I'm suspecting! Fairly even distribution too...someone's been pretty steady and calculated here'

'It's deliberate alright'

'It's disgusting'

'We better check the immediate area for any clues as to who could have done this...maybe even find the weapon used'

They split up and began a rudimental search of the surrounding woodland.

They had been searching for around ten minutes when one of them noticed a similarity before him, and briefly thought that he had lost his way and had been walking around in circles. He looked again. *No, this is new*:

'Sergeant!'

The sergeant heard the urgency in the voice and followed the direction his colleague's call emanated from - not the easiest thing deep in woodland, where sounds ricochet and bounce off the solid tree trunks and distort your sense of hearing.

He sought the constable out and found him gazing at the ground.

'What??'

'I think we've got another one Serg...'

Chapter Eight

An out of breath sergeant suddenly burst into Kent's office, and briefly startled him. He found the Chief Inspector stood up, gazing out of his window at nothing in particular - and deep in thought.

Simpkins' superior promptly sat back down in the chair at his desk.

'What is it??'

'We've found a body sir'

Kent threw his head up in the air, clapped his hands - and rubbed them together enthusiastically. He stood back up and started circling the room:

'Excellent! And so the case moves on at pace. We'll have this one cracked in no time!'

'Errr, Chief Inspector'

Kent noticed the sergeant was not sharing in his enthusiasm. His smile and demeanour waned:

'What??'

'It won't be *quite* as straightforward as that'

'Oh, and why not Simpkins - please do enlighten me?'

'Well...this one's got both its eyes intact Chief Inspector!...'

***

This time, the lay-by outside *Rowley Woods* was full and the lane was full too, but the police had cordoned it off beyond the lay-by, and erected *Police Incident/Diversion* signage.

The police were there in large numbers - a sizeable contingent of regular officers, swelled in number with the presence of a forensics team, dog handlers, a police surgeon and a police photographer.

Kent's driver got him as near to the woods entrance as he physically could and switched off the engine. The Chief Inspector stepped out of the car and strode over to one of his right-hand men. They nodded to each other.

'Right - let's see what we're dealing with first then please, and then you can bring me up to speed with what we've managed to establish to date'

'Certainly sir. Which body or grave would you like to see first Chief Inspector?'

'Are they not together??'

'Errr, no sir'

'Oh! Well...the human remains first then - obviously!'

'Quite so sir...follow me please'

He led the Chief Inspector through a now well-trodden series of twists and turns through mature trees and undergrowth, to a hive of activity centred around the discovery of the human body.

Kent looked down at a body in the early stages of decomposition and putrefaction. The body had been laid out in an unzipped body bag by his men, and placed next to the shallow grave from which it had just been carefully exhumed.

'Do we know who he is?'

'Not yet sir...there's no identification papers or otherwise about his person'

'Well, we'll get straight on to local missing persons then'

'Right sir'

'...especially dog owners'

'Right'

'Oh...and other local dog-walkers who aren't missing too. They may know or recognise who regularly walks their dog or dogs in here!'

'Sure'

The subordinate rapidly scribbled notes as his superior dictated strategy.

'And how did we find it before we removed the chap??'

'Well you'll see the photographs soon enough sir...the police photographer has been snapping away ever since he got here (as they do), but I can say that the loose earth at both shallow graves had been covered over with freshly-broken ferns.

But for the inquisitive dog, both graves may have gone undetected for some time I guess - especially when Autumn comes around and the trees shed a carpet of fallen leaves'

'Yes, there plenty of ferns around alright. Who knows what you could conceal in here!'

'Quite so sir'

The tall policeman bent down to take a closer look at the man. He rolled the body bag slightly, to get a better look at what had killed the man:

'These wounds then...what do we know about them?'

'Deep enough (we reckon) for instantaneous death...he shouldn't have suffered much'

'No...I guess not'

'And there's something else sir'

'Oh yeah?'

'Yes...well, when the dog was found sir, our men initially thought that it had been stabbed three times with the same sharp implement...'

Kent was impatient:

'*But*??'

'But when we found the man here...we found the same three wounds again. We're now convinced that both were stabbed with a three-pronged weapon, approximately seven inches in length. We should, therefore, be able to establish the order of killing once we analyse the bloods - one body will likely have been contaminated with the blood of the other'

'Clever yes! And the dog then??'

'This way sir'

Kent followed his subordinate through what he estimated must have been a good hundred metres or so of undergrowth to the second grave.

Again he looked down, but this time at a very different corpse - and not the type he had to view from time to time on the saddest and most distressing days of his chosen profession.

'A *Yorky* right??'

'That's right sir - a *Yorkshire Terrier*'

'And I hear another dog found this dog here??'

'Correct sir...guess it could smell *one of it's kind*'

'Another *Yorky*??'

'No - but you know what dogs are like...always sniffing each other!'

'Right. Well you can take them both away now'

'Righto sir

One of his men carefully zipped a body bag shut around the small grey and tan dog and prepared to remove it from the woods. A twig snapped nearby, and one of his men came hurrying through the undergrowth looking animated.

The Chief Inspector looked his way:

'What is it??'

'We've found the package label Chief Inspector'

'Excellent - where was it?

'At the premises of one of the maroon car chaps sir'

'I knew it...'

***

Kent and his men arrived mob-handed and parked up outside the offices of *Latchford & Co.* They attracted one or two gawping stares from curious shoppers and passers-by, but largely ignored them and proceeded to enter the premises.

'Geoffrey Wright??'

The question was aimed at the female receptionist. She started to point up the stairs but didn't have time to get any accompanying words out.

With their usual efficiency - and no-nonsense approach to these matters, they quickly by-passed the flustered receptionist and made their way to Geoffrey Wright's office.

It was an entirely disproportionate deployment of resource - given the little trouble they were expecting or envisaged, but Kent was furious. Furious at being *led a merry dance*...and furious that his men were now playing catch-up as a result.

They found their *person of significant interest* perusing accounts at his desk.

'Geoffrey Wright! I'm am charging you with attempting to conceal evidence from the police, and pervert the course of justice. You do not have to say anything. But it may harm your defence if you do not mention when questioned, something which you later rely on in court. Anything you do say will be taken down and may be given in evidence. Do you understand?'

Geoffrey Wright nodded and dropped his head into his hands, crestfallen...

Chapter Nine

Chief Inspector Kent, and one other, sat facing him on the opposite side of the table. They looked deadly serious.

He had refused legal representation (probably an oversight he knew) and wanted to *keep his cards close to his chest* for now. If things got really sticky he could always keep shtum, and contact his solicitor later. He'd back his own judgement in assessing the seriousness of his predicament for now.

'So where's the rest of the body?' the surly-faced Chief Inspector began politely.

'I don't know that I'm afraid'

The Chief Inspector looked at him thoughtfully for a few seconds and remained silent. Certain he wasn't going to offer anything further, he tried again:

'Can't recall? Or you don't know exactly where the body - or body parts, have been dispersed to by now??'

'I'm an innocent party here - I'm not storing a body anywhere, nor trying to get rid of one either!'

'It didn't look like that the other morning, did it, sir? Should we be searching the countryside, quarry holes and landfill sites for miles around??'

'I don't know. I swear I don't know anything about a body - or its whereabouts. Just the eye!'

The Chief Inspector placed a horrible photograph on the desk in front of him, folded his arms - indicating his disapproval...and began his next angle of strategy and questioning:

'So whose eye is this then Mr. Wright?'

He'd seen the real thing of course, but he played the game and looked at the photo presented before him for his viewing. He shook his head:

'I've no idea'

'Really! You've really no idea whose eyeball this is?'

'No...no idea at all'

'You didn't clumsily prise it out of its socket with a screwdriver by any chance??'

'No of course not!...is that what's happened?'

The Chief Inspector just stared at him - trying to read him. There was a long pause.

'Well I don't believe you, sir'

'I swear - really I don't know anything about it, and I didn't do this horrible thing to anyone'

'So why did you take great pains, sir, to take it out on a *joyride* with yourself...well off the beaten track, and off your normal commute to work I might add - and discard the thing off a canal bridge??'

He'd prepared for this one:

'I just wanted to be rid of the thing...it's horrible'

'I'll give you that sir...I'll give you that. Ok, have it your way - who sent you this eyeball then sir?'

Not so prepared this time. He thought fast:

'I don't know...someone with a bizarre and twisted sense of humour. A nutter I expect!'

'A nutter?? I see. You think we're looking for a nutter then sir?'

'Well...I do I expect. Yes'

'Do you know any sir??'

'No I don't...I try to stay well clear of them'

'Don't we all sir. Don't we all. The problem I've got, sir, is that I'm pretty certain that even if *you* think you've been sent this as a nasty and tasteless prank, somebody (as yet unknown maybe) will have sent this specifically to you for some *specific* (maybe warped) reason of their own. So I ask you again...who might have sent you this sir?'

Geoffrey Wright shook his head:

'I don't know. It doesn't make any sense!'

'Oh come on man! There must be someone in your recent past...maybe historic even, who's victim or culprit here. So please think man!'

'I can't...I'm sorry - my head's spinning'

'It was posted in *Folestree Parva,* sir!'

'Folestree Parva??'

'Yes, sir. Have you been there recently?'

'No. No, I haven't'

'Do you know anyone from there then sir?'

'I don't...sorry'

'Sure about that??'

'I'm sure. Sorry'

'You're doing a lot of apologising sir, for one so innocent'

Geoffrey Wright shifted awkwardly in his chair.

There was a knock on the door. It opened and a head popped round:

'They're ready sir'

Kent looked at the door, and then at Geoffrey Wright:

'Excuse me a moment sir'

The tall policeman got up and met his colleague at the door, he murmured something out of earshot, collected something from him, briefly perused it - and returned to the table. He placed it on the table and turned it around so that Geoffrey Wright could view it the right way up.

'Do you recognise this man, sir?'

Geoffrey Wright looked down at a photograph of a man with his eyes closed. *Was he asleep?? No, of course not, stupid...he was dead!*

He studied the photograph carefully and tried to recall. He shook his head.

'You've never met him??'

'No...'

Chapter Ten

'MERV!'

It was Wednesday 17th July. Davieson popped his head out of the kitchen and looked back towards the offices at *The Morning Chronicle:*

'Huh?'

'There you are'

'Hi, Justine. What's up?'

'Chief Inspector Kent on the phone for you Merv...says it's urgent'

The Welshman put his empty mug on the side and carefully tipped the teaspoonful of coffee granules back into the jar he'd just scooped them from. *Coffee could wait - the Chief Inspector couldn't!*

'Thank you...I'm on my way'

He marched off - as fast as his legs would carry him without breaking into a trot, and grabbed his phone:

'Chief Inspector'

'Hello Davieson'

'What can I do for you?'

'We've had a couple of errr...*newsworthy* developments!'

'Newsworthy eh? Go on...'

'The two aren't necessarily connected of course'

'Ok. *And they are*??'

'We've a body for one'

'That's quick - your boys have done well Chief Inspector!'

'There's complications Davieson'

'Oh??'

'Not over the phone...can we meet up, please? I want to bounce things off you again - ask for your take on things. I like our little *walk-and-talks*'

Davieson smiled:

'Of course Chief Inspector...my pleasure. But you said there were a *couple* of developments??'

'Yes. A gentleman is helping us with our enquiries'

'I see. Well - where do you want to meet up then?'

'*Rowley Woods, Upper Woodleigh*. There's a lay-by outside the entrance to the woods. Meet me there please'

'How soon??'

'Can you do now Davieson?'

'I can indeed, Chief Inspector. I'll leave now'

'That'd be grand...'

***

Just the cricket club this side then.

Davieson had looked *Rowley Woods* up on the map, and headed there from the *Morning Chronicle* offices, but there was no obvious lay-by on this side of the woods, no obvious footpath into the woods either...and no sign of Kent!

He decided to drive on and circumnavigate the woods as best as the roads and lanes would allow.

The decision paid off and on the other side of the woods he found Kent parked up in a lay-by. The tall detective was already out of his car and resting against it. Davieson nodded at him, parked up - and got out of his own vehicle:

'Took a bit longer to find than I thought it would sorry. Have you been here long Chief Inspector?'

'Only five minutes Davieson - it's fine'

'Ok...well, show me the way'

Davieson attentively followed the Chief Inspector's every step, mentally noting the lie of the woods and anything suggestive. He was led to a taped-off, open shallow grave and Kent pointed down into it:

'Well, that's where we found the man!'

Kent's intonation suggested there might be more.

'Did you find something else Chief Inspector?'

'Errr, yes - a dog...a *Yorkshire Terrier*'

Davieson frowned:

'Oh...well that's different - something inciteful and emotive for our animal-rights readership at least'

'Quite' said Kent.

'Nevermind. This chap then...who is he?'

'We don't know'

'You don't know??'

'No. No wallet on him, no keys on him, no other form of identification to go on'

'Bad luck. *Anything* on him at all??'

'Very little - just a dog leash in his coat pocket. That's it I'm afraid'

'What did he look like?'

Kent reached into his mac pocket and pulled out a prepared photograph:

'I know you're not squeamish Davieson. He looked like this'

Kent handed the Welshman the *as found when the soil was removed* official police photograph, and the latter studied it thoughtfully.

'Not hit on the head then!'

'The head - no...he was *perforated*!'

'*Perforated??*'

Davieson looked confused.

'Yes - he was run-through with a three-pronged weapon!'

'Like a garden fork??'

'Maybe...maybe you're right there. Very sharp though...so the surgeon tells me'

Kent produced a notepad and scribbled something down.

'And where did you find the dog?'

'*The dog*?? This way'

Davieson again followed the detective through the undergrowth to the second grave. He peered down into a smaller grave, glanced back the way they had just come from...and then finally back at where the dog had been discovered:

'It's some distance away!'

'It is indeed Davieson. Killed with the same implement though...*after* the chap was murdered'

'I see'

Davieson looked around the immediate area and pointed down at his own indistinct footprints:

'Any mileage in the old footprints factor??'

'I'm afraid not Davieson. Footfall in these woods is considerable by all accounts - popular with dog walkers, ramblers and joggers alike. But it's also been a really dry summer. There's therefore little by way of fresh *unique* footprints to go on - and even those that you can discern, account for little more than a plethora of overlapping walking boot, *Wellington* boot and running trainer prints! It'd be like sifting through the layers of an archaeological tell...and we don't have either the time, resources - or patience of *Howard Carter* I'm afraid!'

'*Carter*??'

'Took him ten years to empty and catalogue the contents of *Tutankhamun*'s tomb Davieson'

'Oh, I see'

He lied.

72

'And a gentleman is helping you with your enquiries??'

'Yes. Nothing to do with here, so to speak...we've managed to find the chap who threw the eyeball off the canal bridge'

'Good work! Who is it?'

'One Geoffrey Wright'

'What does he have to say for himself?'

'Not a lot. Swears he knows nothing about it and feels he's the victim of a macabre prank!'

'That doesn't sound very credible'

'No, I agree'

'Fingerprint progress??'

'Well, including the label which Mr. Wright had removed, only his own fingerprints on the label - and only the cyclist's prints on the package itself. Oh, and we also now know from where it was posted, too'

'Where was that?'

'*Folestree Parva* post office. We reckon a girl who works part-time would likely have served the person who sent the parcel, but we're yet to interview her - she's been on a short holiday to the coast'

'Well there could be something there - will you let me know what she says when you've managed to speak with her please?'

'We will indeed Davieson'

'Thank you...and can I write any update yet Chief Inspector?'

'You can indeed....just keep it factual, please. We've found a body, a man is helping us with enquiries (keep Mr. Wright's name out of it for now)...that sort of thing. Someone - or some people, should be missing these two *person's unknown*, and the public (your readership) may well help us there, so I'm keen for you to go to press on these points!'

'Missing these *three*, Chief Inspector!'

'*Three*??'

'Yes - the *Yorkshire Terrier*'

'Oh...of course'

Davieson laughed:

'I'm teasing you sorry. Anyway, my editor will be delighted, so if we're done here - I'll get back to the office and start writing up'

'We're done here yes...it's this way back'

The Chief Inspector led the two men back towards the lay-by. They were almost out of the woods when the Welshman ground to a halt. He looked thoughtful.

'There's one other interesting factor here, Chief Inspector'

'What's that Davieson?'

'Look around you'

The tall policeman looked around but saw nothing but trees and undergrowth:

'I don't follow, sorry'

Davieson looked pleased with himself:

'Everywhere you look, we're surrounded by column after column of mature tree trunks...and of considerable girth too, I might add. Plenty of soft undergrowth growing all around too...perfect for softening your footstep, and insulating any sound we might make. Yes, these woods are absolutely ideal for an ambush Chief Inspector, and perfect for a would-be murderer to take their victim by complete surprise!...'

***

His contribution at work had been terrible - the relentless police visits, series of questioning, and finally the experience of having been grilled and interrogated at length in a police interview room preying heavily on his mind, and disrupting any concentration or focus he might have hoped for.

He'd willed the hours away at work and left the office as early as he practically could. He could sense that colleagues were constantly eyeing him suspiciously, and he could hear the incessant whisperings a mile off.

Back home, Geoffrey Wright got out of his car, opened the front door and checked for the day's post.

Looking down (as he always did) he involuntarily dropped his briefcase with a thud. It narrowly missed his foot.

There had only been one item delivered whilst he had been at work - and to his horror, it was another package. It was much smaller this time, but again his name was printed on the top of it, in a similar fashion to that on the former package.

With a sense of foreboding, he stooped down to pick the package up.

He took it straight through to his kitchen - the tension unbearable, and carefully opened it with a knife.

He took a deep breath, tipped the package gently onto its side - and shook out its contents. A feeling of revulsion swept over him.

It was a bloodied tooth...

Chapter Eleven

The phone rang:
 'Chief Inspector?'
 'Yes, what is it?'
 'We've a Geoffrey Wright asking for you at the front desk downstairs sir. Says he needs to speak to you'
 'Does he now! Right...I'm on my way down'
 Well, well, well - he's come here has he...saves picking him up again ourselves.
 Maybe assumptive - maybe all part of the mind games he would now deploy, but Chief Inspector Kent quite deliberately led his visitor into the same interview room in which he had grilled him at length, on the latter's last visit to *Police Headquarters*.
 'Take a seat sir...you know the one'
 Geoffrey Wright swallowed nervously and sat himself down in a familiar chair, as another policeman joined Kent on *their* side of the desk. He

felt the colour drain from his face and was sure he now looked deathly white.

'Thank you'

'Now then sir. I believe you need to speak to me'

'That's right. I, errr...received another one'

He reached into his pocket and placed a small package on the desk in front of the two policemen. Kent's eyes nearly popped out of his head:

'You can't fit an eye in that. Have you squashed it??'

'*An eye?*? No - no I haven't....it's a tooth'

'*A tooth*??'

'That's right'

'Is someone being taken apart piece by piece?'

He put his head in his hands and shook it frustratingly:

'I don't know'

'Are we to expect dismemberment and larger packages to follow then sir?'

Kent tone was stern, his arms tightly crossed - and the volume of his voice growing ever louder. He stood up:

'Should I have my men stood by to intercept all freight couriers operating in the locality - and have them impound their cargoes perhaps??'

'I've no idea. I've really no idea how their mind may be working...but I *might* know what this is about'

Kent sat back down, and leaned excitedly over the desk in keen interest:

'Oh, you do now do you? Have you upset someone at work Mr. Wright? We understand that there's a sensitive acquisition underway - and that your work is paramount to the offer price on the table, as it were...you're not selling someone short, are you, sir??'

'The acquisition?? No...not at all. I've scrutinised the figures, the balance sheet, assets and liabilities and so on. It's a fair and credible price...my advice and recommendations are sound!'

'What then, what's with this eye and tooth do you suppose?'

'I don't think it's work related at all...even though this current business is emotive and commercially sensitive. No, I think this might be to do with what you might call a hobby or pastime of mine!'

'A *pastime*??'

'Yes - cricket'

'*Cricket*??'

'Yes, there was an awful accident a couple of years ago. Chap copped a fast delivery straight in the face. Sickening it was - he wasn't wearing a helmet you see...'

'And what exactly has that got to do with you then sir'

'Well I don't do it now...the event has put me off for life I'm afraid, but on weekends I used to officiate. I used to love it. I was the, errr, umpire that terrible day'

'And what happened to the chap who came a cropper?'

'I don't know - they carted him off in an ambulance, bleeding profusely. I could barely look at him, it was so awful'

'Was he hit in the eye?'

'I don't know Chief Inspector...maybe'

'Was he hit in the teeth'

'Maybe - certainly the face, yes!'

'Are you somehow to blame then sir?? I'm not entirely following...'

'Some might say that'

'*Some might say?* In what way??'

'The light was poor. I think some were saying afterwards that we never should have continued playing in such bad light. The reality is though, that others were quite bullish and intimidating - and adamant they should play on and try and achieve a result! I had the power to stop play, due to bad light, but I wasn't a strong enough character I'm afraid and succumbed to pressure'

'And where did this match take place, sir?'

'*Upper Woodleigh*. It was *Upper Woodleigh Cricket Club* vs. some opponents whose name escapes me at the present...but it was the *Haverton & District Cricket League*, I can tell you that much'

Kent and his colleague turned to look at each other briefly in silence, then returned their attention to Geoffrey Wright'

'We need to take down particulars of everything you recall sir. Names, when, who said what...'

***

'Davieson'

'Chief Inspector'

'So, we've got a, errr tooth'

The Welshman grabbed his notepad and a nearby pencil:

'A tooth??'

'Yes, a tooth'

'Same *willing donor*?'

Chief Inspector Kent ignored the dark humour.

'We'll be establishing that pronto...well attempting to at least - dental identification isn't always possible you understand?'

'I believe not, no' lied Davieson - *he learnt something new every day in his profession*: 'Was the item dumped again??'

'No, Mr. Wright came to us this time with an *I've received another one storyline*'

'Interesting!'

'It certainly is...hence my call to bring you right up to speed'

'Where posted?'

'Same place - *Folestree Parva*'

'I see. Do you know what this is about yet?'

'Maybe we do actually - and you'll like this...'

'Go on!'

'Mr. Wright thinks it might all revolve around a cricket match'

'*Cricket!* Excellent - it legitimises me mixing business with pleasure then'

Kent chuckled. He knew that Davieson liked his cricket and would watch a match whenever he could. When he couldn't, he'd be tuning into *ball-by-ball* commentary, throughout the summer months, on *Test Match Special*.

'So write away *to your hearts content* my friend. Someone must be missing *someone* somewhere, and publicity might help draw out who should be around and isn't'

'I see your logic Chief Inspector. Anyway, anyone missing the chap in the woods yet?'

There was a pause. *Was Kent frustrated??*

'No. No news there. He might have been a loner, of course, might have been a single chap with few friends or relatives too. Or...'

'Or what Chief Inspector?'

'Or the neighbourhood has closed ranks and is keeping quiet Davieson...'

Chapter Twelve

Her father pulled over as near as he could manage to save his daughter's legs. She thanked him, jumped out of the car and waved goodbye.

A short walk down the pavement, and she entered her workplace to start her Thursday morning shift.

Her boss had already opened up and was straightening tin cans on a shelf. He looked up as she entered the post office. He had an odd, unfathomable, look on his face:

'Morning Mandy. Good holiday??'

Mandy smiled:

'Yes, it was lovely thanks'

'Good. Well, the police are here! They, errr...would like a word with you'

'The *police??*'

He nodded over to his right. Mandy turned her head and noticed two other men in the post office for the first time. There was just the four of them in there...no one else, but until then she had thought that there were only the two of them. It unsettled her somewhat.

'Good morning madam. It shouldn't take too long'

'...And I'll cover things whilst you speak to them, so don't fret there' offered the postmaster.

She shrugged her shoulders:

'So what would you like to talk to me about?'

'This way please, madam'

She was led out the back, which Chief Inspector Kent and his colleague had temporarily commandeered for their interview purposes.

'Have I done something?'

'Kind of...but nothing wrong, we assure you of that'

Chief Inspector Kent's colleague handed his superior two items. They were both entombed in clear evidence bags:

'It all revolves around these madam. One is a package posted here - in a transaction we believe that was administered by yourself. The other is the postage label in question, which became detached from the package at some juncture'

'And??...'

'And we'd like you to try and remember who deposited this for posting please madam' snapped Kent sternly.

'I can't remember specifics of every parcel or package posted here, sorry'

'Well, how many packages do you take in here? It's a village - rather than a town or city centre post office, so it can't be too many surely??'

'Well no' she conceded: '...just a few parcels a day I guess'

'And we can help you narrow things down further' offered Kent: '...it was posted last Monday'

'Ah - now Monday is one of our busier days. Folks planning what they need posting over the weekend, then getting on to it on the Monday, when the post office reopens'

Chief Inspector Kent nodded impatiently, then held the bag containing the label up closer to her face:

'Does this label ring any bells madam?'

She looked at it keenly, then shook her head:

'Well I can see that it's *printed*, rather than in handwriting - but a fair few of our customers do that nowadays...makes the address clearer for the postman, and helps reduce deliveries to the wrong address and the resulting complaints. Some customer's handwriting is atrocious and virtually unreadable!'

'You should see my doctor's prescription notes' laughed Kent - his mood lifting momentarily: 'But do you remember who gave you this particular combination?'

Mandy perused it at length, trying to recall that particular Monday shift. There was an uncomfortable silence whilst the two policemen politely indulged her. Finally, she spoke:

'You have to understand that I haven't worked here that long'

Kent smiled:

'That's quite alright'

'...So I don't as yet know our regular customers as well as my boss out there'

The two policemen briefly looked back at where the postmaster was apparently busying himself, but evidently trying his hardest to discreetly eavesdrop...something they encountered frequently in their line of duty.

'That's alright'

'And he covered my lunch - but I served the rest of the customers that day'

'*And??*'

'...And I think I served a mixture of men and women that day. Some buying stamps, some leaving items for posting, others buying their new fishing licenses...'

'But who do you *think* gave you this parcel please?'

She looked apologetic and pleading:

'I'm sorry - I don't recall'

'Are you sure madam? Please think!'

Kent looked dejected.

'I'm sorry. I can't remember...I've been on holiday since then you know'

'We know that madam. Anywhere nice??'

'A few days at the coast. It was lovely!'

'Yes, you certainly picked a good week for it. Look - we believe this person came back a second time, whilst you were on that holiday. Your boss must have served this person then but...his, errr, memory seems to have failed him - as has your own, so we need all the help we can get if you do recall anything. Whatever the hour - please get in touch'

'I will' she promised.

'...Especially as we likely have *three* dead bodies on her hands'

She looked shocked and fell silent.

Kent didn't let on that one of the three was a dog. He stood up and marched back out into the customer area and the main body of the post office, leaving her standing there in a trance. The postmaster looked up excitedly and Kent addressed him:

'Well thank you for your time. You've *both* been most helpful'

Both Mandy and the postmaster were pretty sure that Chief Inspector Kent was being sarcastic...

***

John Middleton's house phone rang. His wife was nearest to the handset and so promptly answered it:

'Hello'

'Hello, madam. I was after John Middleton'

She detected a Welsh lilt on the other end:

'He's my husband, wait a minute, please. JOHN!'

Davieson could hear somebody approach the telephone handset in the background'

'...There's a man asking after you'

He grabbed the receiver:

'Hello. John Middleton speaking'

'Hello, Mr. Middleton. I believe that you are the current Chairman of *Upper Woodleigh Cricket Club?*'

'That's right. How can I help you?'

'Well I'm writing a piece for the newspaper, and I wondered who kept all the historical records for your club?'

'Cricket fan are you??'

'I am indeed sir. I've watched *Glamorgan* play many a time over the years...but I like my cricket (whatever the standard), grass-roots through to the very best sides'

'Well...we're a *rather good* side ourselves you know?'

'Oh...I'm sure you are sir - I didn't mean to offend you...'

John Middleton chuckled:

'Relax - I'm having a little joke with you...that's all'

'Oh, I see. Good one!'

'Anyway. Alan Chambers - our secretary, is your man. He keeps all the facts and figures, players past and present, match scorecards and such like'

'Excellent! Exactly what I'm after. And how can I get hold of Alan then please?'

'I'll get you his phone number. Hold on a moment please'

Davieson waited...

***

The traffic warden strolled along the street in *Folestree Parva*. It had been a quiet day so far - with little to do as he patrolled the village.

He approached the blue car parked on double-yellow lines outside the post office and scratched his head, a look of bemusement spread over his face.

He peered over the windscreen to check that he wasn't confusing himself - but no...he was right. He'd ticketed the car already. *Had the idiot parked there again - or simply not moved it yet??*

Either way - he or she was getting a fresh ticket today for further (or continued) infringement of parking regulations. He wouldn't be popular, no doubt...these things were expensive, but *rules is rules* as they say - well some folk said it that way anyway...he was sure it should be *rules are rules* by rights.

He affixed a fresh parking ticket to the windscreen with a fair old slap. Completed his paperwork...and walked on...

Chapter Thirteen

Davieson found himself driving once more past the western extremity of *Rowley Woods*. This time he turned into the cricket club and parked up near the pavilion.

A man appeared from out of the building and headed towards his car. Davieson stepped out of his car, just as the man arrived and offered his hand:

'*Alan Chambers???*'

'That's right'

The Welshman shook his hand warmly:

'Merv Davieson - *The Morning Chronicle*. Thank you for agreeing to meet me sir - I'm much obliged'

Alan Chambers smiled:

'Don't mention it...it's my pleasure. I understand that you're writing an article about our club here?'

'I am yes'

'Excellent. We rarely make *the dailies,* so it'd be great to see us in a proper newspaper for a change. Well, I suggested we met here, as this is where we keep the records and old team photographs'

'History and background are an excellent start' agreed Davieson.

'Well, let's start in the bar then...you'll see that we've managed to fill *almost* all of the available wall space in there with framed photographs, certificates and old programmes. It also houses our extensive trophy cabinet, and I *always* enjoy showing visitors (opposing visiting teams or otherwise) the substantial silverware we've managed to achieve and amass over the decades'

Davieson smiled - his host's enthusiasm was infectious:

'And quite right too'

Alan Chambers chuckled:

'Are you a cricket fan yourself?'

'I am sir. *Glamorgan's* my team, although I enjoy following the England Test side too...particularly when they occasionally select a Welshman'

He laughed again:

'I thought you hailed from that neck of the woods...they've had some good teams over the years – *Glamorgan*, that is. Anyway - follow me please'

He led the journalist into the pavilion that had been the headquarters and base of *Upper Woodleigh Cricket Club* for more years than anyone could remember. Davieson loved its *olde-worlde* style. He felt nostalgic and truly in his element.

They proceeded down a couple of corridors towards the clubhouse bar. Every wall was indeed adorned with curios, pennants, prints and photographs - a treasure trove for cricket enthusiasts.

In the bar, another man was stocking a fridge with bottles of beer. Alan Chambers nodded to him as the two entered. Davieson made straight for a gilt-framed sepia photograph, showing two rows of Victorian gentleman sporting matching blazers, and sat behind an impressive (and sizeable) trophy.

Alan Chambers followed his eye:

'Ah - the famed side of 1892!'

'Bit special were they?'

'They were indeed. Went undefeated for quite some time, by all accounts. And here's the trophy in question...Cost's us a fortune in insurance mind!'

The Welshman followed his host to a locked glass trophy cabinet. Taking pride of place on the bottom shelf was the antique silverware in question, decorated with vintage ribbons (*he assumed in the colours of Upper Woodleigh Cricket Club*).

'It was a regional competition that had ceased by the time Edward VII came to the throne. We won the inaugural trophy – that's the photograph you see back there, and we won its final staging too...so they rightly let us keep it!'

"Oh of course' agreed Davieson.

'And here are our honours boards'

Davieson again followed his host to two large wooden boards, commemorating all the home centuries scored in cricket matches for the club -

and all instances of a home bowler taking five wickets in an innings. He perused the names in keen interest. There were cricketers who had starred for a decade or more - and hints of sporting dynasties, a common occurrence in tight-knit village cricket teams where youngsters would often follow in the footsteps of father and grandfather.

'Forgive me - I should offer you a drink first anyway. Anything I can get you from our amply-stocked bar??'

'Any of your real ales would be lovely thanks. Do you mind if I make some notes here?'

'Not at all. I'll get the drinks'

Davieson sat himself down in a comfy chair.

Alan Chambers reached for his wallet and strode over to the bar - leaving the journalist scribbling away in his notepad. He attracted the attention of the barman, Bob, and ordered two pints of real ale.

He returned just as the Welshman looked up from his pad:

'Some notable successes, and some fine batting and bowling figures...but I understand that it's not all been so positive. There was an accident I heard ab...'

'The accident!!'

'Yes. I'm sure there's been more than one over the years though'

'Well yes...but when people mention *the accident*, they generally mean the one that happened a couple of seasons ago'

'What happened?'

His host handed Davieson his pint, sat himself down in a chair facing the Welshman, took a sip of his own beer and began:

'One of our boys...figurative you understand (he was in his forties), copped a ball at pace, straight in the face'

'Messy was it?'

'Messy...it was terrible. The leather casing on a cricket ball rarely comes off second best when it meets with soft tissue!'

'No, I guess not. Who was the unfortunate fellow?'

'Roger...Roger Lenton, our wicket-keeper - or was our wicket-keeper I should say. Shattered his confidence (bless him) and he's never turned out for *Upper Woodleigh* since. We've tried to tease him back from time to time, but he's adamant his cricketing days are well and truly over and done with. It's a crying shame, as he was exceptional with the gloves'

'A shame indeed. Did you witness the accident??'
'Sort of'
'*Sort of??*'

'Well I was scoring that day - from the terrace here at the clubhouse, so I wasn't in the field or near at hand, but I could see enough to know that it must have hurt the chap...and to hear Roger's cries of course. He was wailing like a banshee!'

'What happened exactly?'

'Well...in my humble opinion, a storm was brewing up. I recall the light quickly deteriorating and turning really dark under the covered terrace here...so dark in fact, that I could barely see my scorecard to record properly, and found myself squinting to continue (my eyes aren't what they used to be now I'm afraid)'

'Mine neither...hence these oval-shaped spectacles. I'm near-blind without them I tell you' laughed Davieson.

His host smiled politely, and continued:

'It had already been very cloudy and overcast, to begin with, I might add. I guess the way *Health and Safety* has gone nowadays - we *probably* shouldn't have still been playing...but we did.

It seemed like it was getting progressively harder for the guys to judge the flight of the ball accurately. From the exclamations they were uttering, it looked like a couple of deliveries had already whistled past the opposing batman's ears and then another delivery came in - he bottled it...and promptly ducked.

From *his* perspective, he timed his duck to perfection - but for poor old Roger...well, it meant he copped it straight in the face with no notice whatsoever I'm afraid to say. He didn't stand a chance!'

Davieson winced in sympathy.

'Well, still interesting (if unfortunate). Do you keep in touch with Roger??'

'Roger?? We hardly see him poor fellow, but I look him up every now and then - check he's ok, that sort of thing. We're a tight-knit village side, and you make many good friendships over the years - Roger is still family from that respect and part of *Upper Woodleigh's* history'

'Do you remember much more about the accident itself?

'Well, the umpire did then abandon the match (he had no choice by then). Abandoned due to bad light officially...although no one had the stomach to play on at that stage in proceedings. The ambulance arrived, Roger was carted off - and we all returned home with our spirits dampened'

'Do you have the scorecard here for that fateful match?'

'We will have yes...we retain them all here at the clubhouse'

'Mind if I have a look at it please?'

'Not at all. Give me a minute to find it out and I'll get it for you'

The secretary of *Upper Woodleigh Cricket Club* disappeared off and left Davieson to enjoy his pint and expand the notes he was making.

His host returned a moment or two later and handed him the scorecard. The writing was incredibly neat and easy to discern any detail or statistic a would-be reader would care for.

'Thank you - I'll make a few brief notes, if I may'

Alan Chambers glanced at his watch and then jumped to his feet:

'Of course. Anyway, I've got to shoot I'm afraid, but take your time - Bob will show you out when you've finished your notes and drink'

Davieson stood up himself and shook his hand:

'Thank you Alan - it's been a fascinating morning, so thank you once again for your time and for indulging me. Fabulous club you have here'

'No problem - I'm glad to help. I await your article with keen interest!'

With that, he departed.

Davieson took a gulp of his hoppy pint and wrote some more...

Chapter Fourteen

There was an authoritative knock at the front door.

John Middleton turned his television set off and answered the door. There were a couple of men on his doorstep - one of them, he noted, was very tall. He didn't recognise either of them.

'Mr. Middleton?'

'That's right'

The tall man reached inside his lightweight overcoat and flashed credentials in his face:

'Chief Inspector Kent. May I have a word please?'

'*Ch?*...sure...I guess. Please do come in'

Kent thought he looked genuinely confused. John Middleton waved the two of them in and closed the door behind them. They followed him past an equally bewildered Mrs. Middleton.

'What's this about? *John??*' she enquired, addressing her questions first to the policemen and then quickly to her husband.

Kent took control:

'Nothing to worry about directly madam - we just believe your husband may be able to help us with a case we're investigating'

'Oh...ok' she said unconvincingly: 'What are you investigating?'

'Well - murder madam'

'*Murder??*'

'Yes. A couple of murders actually!'

'Good grief!'

She sat down. Her husband looked as equally shocked as she did. Kent eyed them both keenly.

'Well, what's this got to do with John? I don't understand...'

'Not John directly madam...well they'll be a few formalities to work through, just to eliminate and confirm that - but we have reason to believe that one of these murders concerns *Upper Woodleigh Cricket Club* in some fashion or other'

'The Cricket Club! *John??*'

John Middleton shook his head:

'I've no idea dear...look Chief Inspector, I'm sorry - but I'm still none the wiser as to what you're referring to exactly I'm afraid'

'We understand that you're the chairman of this particular club sir?'

'That's right - but I still don't understand...'

'Well, we understand that there was a serious accident a year or two ago sir'

'*The accident*?? Yes, there was an accident all right...but there was no fatality!'

'Well, there is one now sir...maybe three!'

John Middleton noticeably paled:

'I thought you said a couple?'

'I'm sharing information on a need to know basis sir'

'Yes, of course...sorry'

'No problem sir, but I do need you to tell me everything you can recall about that accident. Whether you witnessed it, names...dates etc.'

'Ok. Well I was watching from the pavilion terrace, in my favourite (and strategically placed) chair...and with an ice-cold gin and tonic in my hand I should imagine'

'Go on' encouraged Kent.

'Well, I recall it went rather dark. It wasn't raining though...well the heavens did open later on to be fair, but not at that stage - no it didn't rain until after the match was abandoned'

'And the accident??'

'Well the ball had been zipping around for a while, and then poor old Roger copped for one'

'Make a note of that please sergeant. Errr, in his face I understand??'

'That's right'

'Pace bowling?'

'I guess so. To be fair, the deliveries all look fast when you're a retired ex-player looking on though. The passing of time I guess. I'm sure I faced worse in my younger playing days!'

'Oh, I'm sure you did sir. And what other players were involved that day?'

'The *others??* Well, one remembers Roger of course...impossible to forget his involvement that day. But the others?...you'll have to speak to our secretary, he collates and archives all the press coverage, scorecards and records'

'And who is that please sir?'

'Alan...Alan Chambers'

'And how do we get in contact with Alan Chambers then please sir?'

'I'll fetch you his details'

He disappeared out of the room, leaving his wife alone with the two policemen. She smiled nervously whilst Kent nodded thoughtfully to himself.

John Middleton returned shortly with handwritten contact details which he offered Kent.

The tall policeman took the scrap of paper, double-checked he could read the handwriting clearly - and slipped it into his pocket.

'Well, good day sir'

The policeman stood up and moved towards the front door. John Middleton followed them, stopped - and suddenly chuckled to himself. His wife had discreetly followed the three of them and now stood quietly behind.

Kent wheeled round:

'Something funny sir??'

'*Funny??* No.. it's just that I guess this murder business is what that journalist was *actually* fishing around for too. He hadn't mentioned exactly why he was writing an article himself'

'*Journalist??*'

'Yes - Welsh fellow'

'Oh him...'

***

'I'll have another of those please - that was lovely'

Davieson placed his empty pint glass back on the bar and reached into his trouser pocket for coins. The barman started to refill it.

'Certainly sir'

'Bob is it??'

'That's right sir. Bob Butler'

'And what do you remember about Roger's accident Bob?...were you here then?'

'I was here alright, but I don't recall too much - and I didn't see the accident itself. I tend to watch snippets of play here and there, nipping out to the terrace when it's quiet - but with half an eye on the bar at all times still...in case anyone wants a refill'

'So you were back here at the time?'

'That's right. I had thought the match was nearly over, and so had come back in here to prepare for a rush of thirsty spectators and players'

'Because the light was failing, and you thought the match would be stopped??'

'*The light??* No - because I had heard from John that it looked like our side had convinced the umpire that we should play on and could achieve the win. It had looked as if a draw was on the cards ever since lunch really, but then there had been a late flurry of wickets, and the result looked possible'

'So you weren't expecting bad light to stop the play??'

'No - not at all. In fact, I can't recall a game ever being abandoned here (up until then) in my living memory. I can remember a couple of occasions where the light had gotten so bad that the players pulled together and drove their cars as near to the boundary as they dare, positioning them like the numbers on a clock face. Then they started their car engines, put full beam on - and floodlight the wicket and outfield as best they could. That got us through the final overs then - but never abandoned, no'

'I see'

Bob Butler set the second pint down in front of Davieson, The latter took a sip, deep in thought.

'Have you seen Roger recently?'

'No. Shame that - he was good company in the bar here, never any aggro...and a good customer'

'Spent a bit behind the bar did he??'

Bob Butler looked confused:

'Sorry - I meant that he was respectful of the club and bar rules, so a good customer from that respect...a model citizen if you like!'

'And some aren't??'

The question threw the barman and he fell silent. Davieson didn't press him.

'Was Roger bitter about the whole thing?'

'I couldn't say - I've barely spoken to him since...it's hard to know what to say to him exactly, you know?'

'I know'

Davieson nodded, took a large quaff of his beer - and again left the discussion hanging. Bob Butler did not offer anything further, however, so he just smiled politely and enjoyed his second pint.

The barman eased away and continued with his duties, leaving the journalist to himself and his thoughts.

When he had finished his pint, Davieson cleared his throat to draw the barman's attention:

'Anyway, I must be heading off now. Thank you'

The journalist set his empty pint glass down once more on the bar and gave the barman a friendly smile.

Bob Butler didn't ask for the loaned scorecard as Davieson turned to leave.

Equally, Davieson did not retrieve it from where he had casually stashed it earlier, whilst the former had been engrossed in his work behind the bar...

Chapter Fifteen

'This is the place, pull over'

The police driver obediently brought the car to a standstill, outside the plain and simple premises of Alan Chambers. Kent and his sergeant jumped out and the two of them proceeded up the drive.

The tall policeman rapped the door and stepped back a pace.

There was no answer. Kent checked his wristwatch, and tried again (a little harder).

Still no answer. He snorted indignantly, and turned to leave:

'We'll try again later'

Just then the homeowner turned into his drive, and Kent's spirits lifted:

'Ah - here he is now'

A look of confusion was evident on Alan Chamber's face. He stared at the two strangers on his doorstep, and stopped:

'Can I help you??'

'Alan Chambers??'

The secretary of *Upper Woodleigh Cricket Club* nodded his head slowly.

Kent conjured up a false smile:

'Well, we believe so sir. Chief Inspector Kent...we'd like a moment of your time please'

'Oh??'

He looked briefly back at the road. It was quiet:

'Well, you best come in then. Can I get you a drink?'

'Two teas, please. Milk in both...three sugars in mine'

The Chief Inspector evidently knew the beverage preference of his subordinate and was well-used to ordering for the both of them.

They followed their host into his home and were directed to a modest lounge. A couple of cricket prints were hung on the wall, as was a framed selection of antique cigarette cards depicting stars of the game from yesteryear. Kent walked up and leant towards it to read the names. He noted W.G. Grace, Donald Bradman and Garfield Sobers were all included.

Alan Chambers returned with three teas. He put one down on a coffee table and handed another to Kent:

'So what's this about gentlemen?'

'We're investigating a couple of murders sir'

'Murders??'

'That's right sir, and a gentleman, *helping us with enquiries,* thinks it might all revolve around your cricket club'

'Upper Woodleigh??'

'That's right sir'

'Well, I don't see how - we're a close-knit village club. We're like one big happy family in fact...have been for years!'

'We understand that there was a nasty accident a couple of year's ago Mr. Chambers?'

Alan Chambers clattered his mug of tea down noisily onto a drinks coaster:

'Good Lord. Roger's not died, has he? I know he'd become irreversibly introvert, and a shadow of his former self- but I thought his physical health overall had improved!'

Kent and his sergeant glanced briefly at each other. Kent decided to overlook the earlier conversation with John Middleton, and grill his new subject afresh - a tactic he would often employ to substantiate or refute others' testimony:

'Who's Roger?'

'Roger...Roger Lenton - an ex-player of ours. It was him involved in the accident...is he alright?'

'We'll find out sir - all in good time'

'I'm not sure how I can help you though'

'We understand that you're the secretary of this cricket club sir?'

'That's right'

'...And that you collate and archive the records'

'I do yes'

'Well we need to see the scorecard pertaining to the match in which that accident happened sir'

'Well I don't keep the records at home here...everything is filed meticulously at the clubhouse'

'No bother sir - we can collect it from wherever it resides'

'You'll actually need to ask for Bob - he's got the scorecard'

'*Bob*??'

'Yes. Bob Butler - our barman there'

'Make a note of that please sergeant...'

***

The curtains were firmly closed.

Was he up yet? Surely he'd be up by now??

Davieson checked his watch. It wasn't particularly early. He tried again...

Success at the second time of trying. He heard a noise inside and presently the door opened. A bleary-eyed man with bedraggled hair stood before him:

'Mr. Lenton??'

The man rubbed his eyes and brow in a circular fashion:

'Errr, yes - that's me'

'Merv Davieson...*The Morning Chronicle*. Can I speak with you please?'

'Come in'

Davieson followed the pyjama-clad homeowner inside. The pyjamas looked grubby, the air smelt stale. He decided to try and gloss over both these points in the line of duty.

'Would you like a cuppa? I've not had a drink myself yet'

Davieson could well believe it:

'No thank you - I've just had a coffee' he lied.

'Mind if I make myself one quickly first?'

'Not at all. Can I take a seat while I wait?'

'Please do'

Davieson took the cleanest seat he could find, whilst Roger Lenton shuffled off to put the kettle on.

He returned with a dubious-looking mug of tea and sat down on a sofa riddled with unopened bills and letters:

'Well, what would you like to speak about?

'It's about these local murders Mr. Lenton'

'*Murders??*'

'Yes - the ones in the news'

'I'm sorry - I don't really watch the news...I've become a bit of a recluse, according to my doctor'

'Well, they're covered in the newspapers too Mr. Lenton - including the paper I write for'

'Oh I'm sorry - I cancelled the papers last year...fed up of reading about other folks happiness, health and wealth'

'I see. Have you always kept yourself to yourself?'

'No, not at all. I used to be out and about all the time, and very sociable - I could look a man in the eye you know?'

A quietness descended on the room. Roger Lenton started rocking gently and Davieson thought he detected a nervous tic, or twitching, involuntarily animating the man's face.

'What happened?...what changed??'

'Lost my confidence, following an accident. It completely changed my former outgoing personality and I sank into a deep, deep depression. I've been on tablets for it ever since...but I'm not sure they're helping me much. I'm sorry...I bet you don't really want to hear about my miserable existence - just feeling a little sorry for myself you know?'

'No problem Mr. Lenton. I'm all ears'

'Anyway. Who's been murdered?'

'Ah yes - the murders. Well, the police, errr - don't know that at present'

'And where do I fit in? Do you want to know if I've seen or heard anything newsworthy?'

'Well, you can probably be a lot more helpful than that Mr.Lenton'

'In what way?'

'Well, there's a theory...just a theory mind, that the murders may relate in some way or other to your accident. I'll confess that I did know that you'd had a nasty accident...but I didn't know the trauma it has obviously put you through, and that it had been so life-changing for you!'

Roger Lenton took a loud slurp of tea. *It was obviously too hot for him (he shouldn't have even attempted it - and probably just a nervous reflex action).*

'My accident' he muttered absently.

'Yes...what do you recall of it?'

'*What do I recall of it??* Well, it was getting pretty dark. A couple of balls whizzed past their batsman...he didn't get anywhere near them, and I safely retrieved them in my gloves, preventing any extras.

The next ball comes in (even faster) - and with zero forewarning, the batsman ducks. I had no time to react and it caught me flush in the face. I was immediately floored - a helpless wreck lying on the deck'

Davieson again winced in sympathy (this time for Roger Lenton's benefit), on hearing about the horrible injury a second time.

'Were you wearing a helmet?'

'Helmet?? Nah...never did. No, I thought my judgement of the flight of the ball was second to none'

'And looking back Mr. Lenton...do you blame anyone for the accident??'

Roger Lenton stood up and moved over to the curtains. He drew them open and stood gazing out of the window - his back turned to Davieson:

'*Do I blame anyone??* Now that's an interesting question. I suppose with the benefit of hindsight, the umpire never should have let us keep playing...or the batsman to continue to face balls I should say! Apart from that, I've considered since that their batsman *bottled it*, and that his ducking bore all the hallmarks of cowardice and self-preservation. The manly and determined thing to do would have been to stand firm, stay strong - and face the damn thing!...'

Chapter Sixteen

'This is the place'

'Righto Chief Inspector'

The police car parked up and Kent and his sergeant stepped out. Kent immediately strode out to the edge of the cricket boundary and looked out over the outfield in admiration:

'Just look at that grass!...it's immaculate. They must have a very good groundsman here - could do with him sorting our lawn out back home. Mrs. Kent would be well pleased with something of this order'

The sergeant laughed politely.

Kent pointed:

'We were searching the woodlands just over there look'

The sergeant looked over towards the scene of the extensive police search that had been undertaken throughout the undergrowth of *Rowley Woods* in the last few days.

'Is the proximity significant sir?'

'It may be sergeant...it may be. Anyway, who left that incident tape on those holly bushes there?'

'Errr - I'm not sure sir, I thought we'd taken it all down. Shall I remove it??'

'Please do sergeant - we don't want to be over alarming the locals now that we've seen what we had to see. I'll be inside'

The sergeant started to walk around the edge of the boundary and off towards *Rowley Woods*, whilst his superior headed into the clubhouse, or pavilion, of *Upper Woodleigh Cricket Club*.

The Chief Inspector found his way through to the bar. There was a man behind the pumps.

'Bob Butler?'

The man nodded:

'That's me'

'Chief Inspector Kent. May I have a word please?'

'Sure'

'We've been speaking with Alan Chambers sir...we've just come from there in fact...'

The barman leant over the bar and peered either side of Kent, he shook his head slightly confused:

'*We??*'

Kent turned around and looked behind him himself:

'Oh sorry, my sergeant's outside - he'll be along here shortly though. Anyway, you have a scorecard we need to borrow please'

'*Scorecard??* Well Alan looks after those - you'll need to speak to him'

'We've just spoken to Alan sir...as I said. He said it's here sir'

'Well it *probably* is - I'm sure Alan must store them here somewhere, but I've no idea where exactly, so (as I say) - you'll need to speak to him'

'He specifically said it was with you, sir!'

Bob Butler shrugged his shoulders:

'Beer mats, optics - packets of peanuts maybe...but not scorecards Chief Inspector. I've no idea why he said that to you...no idea at all'

'You trying to be funny sir?'

The barman flushed scarlet:

'Errr no Chief Inspector...sorry'

'Have you *any* scorecards in your possession or care sir?'

'None'

'Positive?'

'I'm certain Chief Inspector'

'Right. Good day sir!'

The tall policeman wheeled around. Bob Butler thought he looked angry.

The sergeant arrived at the barroom door, just as his superior came bounding through it in the opposite direction. He thought his Chief Inspector looked annoyed.

'We're off Jones...back where we came from, would you believe?'

'Oh - I...'
'I MIGHT BE BACK' yelled Kent for Bob Butler's benefit...

***

Davieson drove out to *Folestree Parva* on the Friday morning, humming an indistinguishable tune absently to himself. The case was continuing to interest him and his spirits soared accordingly.

He found the post office easy enough, and parked his car just behind a stationary, and empty, blue vehicle. He tutted at the laziness of those individuals who insisted in parking as few inches away from their target destination, or shop, as possible...even if that meant parking illegally, dangerously - or both!

He got out, locked his car and entered the post office. There was a man being served by a young girl at the counter. *The owner of the blue car inconveniencing others no doubt.*

Davieson decided to keep his private thoughts to himself. An argument wouldn't aid his course. He instead waited patiently until the man had been served and departed the post office.

He and the young girl were now alone and this was likely to be the most productive opportunity. He approached the counter.

'Hello sir'

'Hello there. I'd like a book of first class stamps, please'

'Sure'

The girl opened a drawer behind the counter and pulled out a pile of books of stamps, bound with an elastic band. She removed the top book and passed it over to Davieson. Davieson placed sufficient coins down on the counter, retrieved his change, filed the stamps away in his blazer pocket - and smiled:

'You heard about these murders?'

The Welshman sounded natural, jovial - unthreatening.

The girl's eyes widened. She leant forward conspiratorially and lowered her voice to a whisper. *This was entirely unnecessary...they were still quite alone.*

'*Heard about them??*...It was only me that served the creep you know?'

'*Served the creep* - what do you mean?'

'Well, the police reckon the body parts were posted right here! And one of them whilst I was on duty'

'No!!'

Davieson continued to keep any prior knowledge of further details to himself. She was buying it...

'Yeah! Horrible isn't it?'

'Quite. Bad luck it was on your shift too! Bet you wish it was on someone else's shift eh??'

'Well there's only my boss (the postmaster) and myself, but they think another body part was handed into him for posting too...so I think we got one each, as it happens, unfortunately'

'I see. Well, bad luck the both of you then! I wouldn't wish anyone being caught up in something like that'

'Thank you. I just wish they hadn't chosen this post office to fulfil their twisted intentions'

'I bet you do. Do you, errr - remember who posted it?'

Mandy shook her head apologetically:

'I don't I'm afraid. We can serve all sorts in here on busy days'

The journalist looked about the empty post office. He looked confused:

'Just not today, eh?'

She blushed and felt a little stupid:

'I guess not sir'

'Did the police give you a hard time?'

She huffed and looked resentful:

'A little - I guess. I'm not sure the Chief Inspector was exactly (what you might call) *impressed* with me!'

'Because you couldn't recall who left the parcel for posting??'

'Yeah. He was sarcastic - you know?'

'Oh I know his sort all right' laughed Davieson...*he had witnessed Kent's manner - and the approach he took with his subjects first hand*: 'Can you remember whether it was male or female at least?'

'I can't I'm afraid. I've tried to remember...it's kept me awake at night in fact. But I just can't remember'

The Welshman fumbled in his blazer pocket again and produced two scraps of newspaper. He carefully unfolded them, turned them the right way around and showed them to Mandy:

'It couldn't have been either of these two chaps could it??'

Davieson had acquired the newspaper clippings from the archives of the local newspaper business pages and sports pages. One of them showed a photograph of Geoffrey Wright - the other a cricket team in a traditional pose. Davieson had circled round the face of Roger Lenton in biro. He gave her a moment to peruse them and could envisage the cogs turning in her brain.

She shook her head:

'Maybe...maybe not - I couldn't be sure I'm afraid - here...you're not the police again are you??'

'*The police??* No, no...I'm a journalist. Merv Davieson - *The Morning Chronicle*'

The journalist offered his hand. She wavered for a second or two, and then shook it:

'Pleased to meet you...you seem nice enough!'

Davieson beamed at her warmly:

'Thank you. Anyway - must dash...you've got another customer coming, and I've taken up far too much of your time already'

Mandy looked over his shoulder, as an old lady entered the post office. Davieson returned the newspaper clippings to his pocket and made his departure. He gave the old lady the once-over in passing...*she didn't look like a serial killer.*

Just before the old lady had quite made it to the counter, Mandy shouted over her shoulder (startling her) to catch Davieson's attention before he stepped outside:

'Did you even need the stamps??'

He turned about and tapped his blazer pocket gently:

'They always come in handy madam...always come in handy!'

She smiled:

'Can I help you, madam?...'

Chapter Seventeen

Kent slammed the car door shut with some ferocity, and stormed up the driveway. Sergeant Jones locked the car and raced after him. He only just caught up with his superior as the latter began hammering on the front door of Alan Chambers.

Inside could be heard an:

'Alright, alright, alright'

The door swung open and Alan Chamber's face fell:

'Oh, it's you again'

'It is indeed Mr. Chambers. You've been giving us the runaround!'

'I'm sorry??'

'Wasting police time is a criminal offence you know sir?'

'I know that Chief Inspector - I'm not stupid...and I haven't been wasting your time!'

'You distinctly told us that your barman friend...one *Robert Butler*, had the cricket club scorecards'

'Well not all of them...but the one you asked about, pertaining to the accident - sure'

'He denies having ever been in possession of it sir! Isn't that right Jones?'

The (till-then) quiet sergeant dutifully confirmed that to be the case, although Sergeant Jones hadn't actually had this ratified by Bob Butler himself! Sergeant Jones had not (indeed) had a chance to speak with Bob Butler directly at all- but had instead been subjected to a lengthy tirade from Chief Inspector Kent on the drive over from the cricket club! His superior had colourfully filled him in on *all* particulars, and on what Bob Butler had had to say for himself.

Alan Chambers briefly tapped his head:

'Ah - it must be in the bar'

'*The bar*?? Is that normal'

'Well no - but a journalist had asked about the scorecard too. I sought it out for him, but had to dash off and asked him to leave it with Bob when he had made whatever notes he needed to'

'Which paper was this journalist from sir?'

'*The Morning Chronicle*'

'Welsh fellow??'

'That's right. Do you know the chap?'

'I do indeed sir. Good day'

Kent stormed off. Sergeant Jones looked Alan Chambers briefly in the eye, discreetly smiled at him - and followed. The Chief Inspector was already waiting impatiently at the locked police car as he himself reached the vehicle...

***

'Hello - is it Mr. Ellsmere?'

Craig Ellsmere looked at the Welshman on his doorstep with a degree of curiosity. He'd no idea who his visitor was:

'It is yes - can I help you?'

'Captain of *Upper Woodleigh Cricket Club right??*'

'That's right'

'Excellent. Can I pick your brains then please?'

'Cricket fan are you?

'I am indeed sir - I am indeed'

'Great, well please do come in. Cuppa??'

'I'd love one thanks'

'Coffee ok??'

'That would be grand - thank you'

Davieson took a seat in the lounge whilst Craig Ellsmere switched the kettle on and rattled various crockery in his kitchen. Separated by a narrow hall, the Welshman distinctly heard the unmistakable sound of a biscuit tin opened, rifled through - and closed again. His host returned smiling, armed with two mugs of steaming coffee and a plate of biscuits. He set one of the mugs and the plate down on a coffee table in front of Davieson and found himself a seat:

'Well - pick away'

'The *biscuits??*'

Craig Ellsmere burst into laughter:

'No - my brains!'

'Oh, I see. Right - mind if I make some notes?'

'Not at all'

The journalist produced a biro and spiral-bound notepad from his blazer pocket. He popped a biscuit in his mouth, flicked a few used pages of the notepad over - and found a blank unused one:

'So you're Captain of the 1st XI here then Mr. Ellsmere?'

'That's right, yes'

'And how long have you held the captaincy for?'

Craig Ellsmere thought for a moment:

'It must be half a dozen years or more by now'

'So you would have been Captain when Roger Lenton had his unfortunate accident then?'

Craig Ellsmere looked rueful and sympathetic:

'I was, yes...a terrible day that was!'

'So I hear. Do you, errr - select the 1st XI Mr. Ellsmere?'

'I do yes. We try to keep things simple here - no selection committee complications and having to satisfy *all and sundry*...we do pretty well out of it too!, so the chairman and players alike trust me'

'Yes, I can see *Upper Woodleigh* do very well - so well done there sir!'

Craig Ellsmere blushed, as Davieson tried his coffee:

'Thank you. You're very kind'

'And do you, errr - likewise manage the team during the game?...you know, fielding positions, next bowler etc.?'

'I do yes'

'I understand that when Roger had his accident, some on the pitch (and around) thought that maybe the match should have been abandoned on the grounds of diminishing light?'

'Some did - yes'

'Were you one of them??'

'Not really, no'

'But as Captain, you would have tried to persuade the Umpire to play on...particularly after (I hear) there was a flurry of late wickets, right??'

'Maybe...but I don't recall doing that. Here - you're not managing an insurance claim are you??'

Davieson laughed and beamed at his host:

'No, relax Mr. Ellsmere. I'm a journalist. Merv Davieson - *The Morning Chronicle*'

The Welshman rose, strode across the lounge and offered his hand. Craig Ellsmere took it - still a little wary, but it seemed to break the ice. He sat back down and started his own coffee:

'What - and you're writing a story about Roger's accident??'

'Kind of, yes'

'Oh well, no bother - carry on'

'So do you recall how the Umpire came to allow play to continue?'

'Well, we were at home. I guess he felt pressured because our star bowler had started to knock the stumps down like skittles. We've some quite vocal characters here (he was one of them)...and it looked like he might put them to bed and force the result before the light got any worse'

Davieson reached inside his blazer pocket and produced the scorecard. He looked down it, running his finger slowly down the sequence of scoring whilst he sipped his mug absently:

'That bowler who *got his eye in* (as they say) so late in the game - despite poor visibility, was Peter Chapman right?'

Craig Ellsmere nodded:

'Peter, yes'

Davieson made a note, his visualisation of the historic sequence of events improving with each new perspective he heard:

'Had your opponents asked the Umpire to end things?'

'There were grumbles certainly...but I think they largely fell on deaf ears amongst the vociferous counter-argument from ourselves'

'So they were shouted down, in a partisan atmosphere, would you say??'

'Errr...I guess so yes'

Davieson stood up.

'Well thank you sir...and thank you for the coffee and biscuits - I won't take any more of your time'

The journalist downed his coffee and set the empty mug down.

'No problem'

Craig Ellsmere showed the journalist to the door and let him out. He closed the door behind him. He was worried that he might about to be directly quoted in the following morning's *Morning Chronicle*, and felt sure that - in the context of his discussion with the journalist, that might bring trouble (in some form or other) for his beloved cricket club...

Chapter Eighteen

The village was right over the other side of the county - and not blessed with the widest choice of transport links, but it was a glorious day and Davieson enjoyed a drive in the country, whether it be a journey of considerable length - or simply popping out to a convenience store to stock up with cigarettes.

He'd researched the place as best he could, and drove as slowly as he could get away with (without risking hampering anyone following him) once he reached the village - until he found the property he was after.

Fortunately, it was a quiet day, and he didn't need to hold any vehicles up behind him, whilst he methodically counted the house numbers down.

Having parked up outside the intended property and locked the car, he ambled up the drive and rapped the door, checking the name on the scorecard once again. Davieson put it back in his blazer pocket just before the door opened:

'*David Heath??*'

'It is, yes'

'Hello. I believe you are (or were) Captain of *Charnford Cricket Club*?'

'That's correct...I still am'

'Excellent. Merv Davieson - *The Morning Chronicle*. May I have a word about a cricketing accident that occurred in a game that you were participating in please?'

'Oh, that!...well I tried to prevent it!'

Davieson smiled slowly and politely:

'So...may we talk??'

'Yes of course, please do come in'

'Thank you'

David Heath led him into a tidy kitchen and offered him a seat, but no drink.

'The accident then. What would you like to know?'

The Welshman took out his notepad and biro from his blazer pocket:

'Recollections really. What you remember of the accident, any characters that stood out...that sort of thing'

'Well - as I said at the time (and I'll say it again now), I thought it was downright dangerous and ridiculous that we were still playing! Our batsman should never have been expected to stay out there in that light, with balls whizzing past his skull. No - *Upper Woodleigh* should have *cut their losses* and accepted the draw. Yes, there were a few late wickets they managed to take - but too little too late....far too late I'm afraid!'

The Captain of *Charnford Cricket Club* had become very animated and a colour tone or two more red. Davieson was enthralled.

'You said that you had tried to prevent it??'

'That's right. Told the umpire exactly what I thought and expressed my concerns for our batsman's safety. I was the non-striking batsman at the bowler's end you see, so I suggested that he needed to *offer us the light*'

'What did he say?'

'Well he didn't get a chance to reply really...the *Upper Woodleigh* greed set in! He was just about to speak when their bowler aborted his run-up, and rounded on the poor umpire. He then proceeded to vent his spleen in such an intimidating fashion that the umpire simply buckled under pressure, turned towards me and informed me that he thought *Upper Woodleigh* could seal the victory in the next over or so and that their bowler had promised him that he'd slow things down a little.

Well - do you know what he did?'

'The bowler?'

'Yes'

Davieson shrugged his shoulders at a loss, but was enjoying giving David Heath plenty of time to get things off his chest. He remained silent and continued to give the Captain of *Charnford Cricket Club* his full attention.

'He only set the field accordingly for a slower delivery didn't he! Fooling his own team-mates as to his actual intentions, would you believe - and showing scant regard for their safety too!

He then comes haring in (faster still by my recollection) like an absolute maniac and, well - our batsman ducked, the ball struck their wicketkeeper...and there was a sickening crack'

The Welshman reached inside his blazer pocket and pretended to reference the scorecard:

'That bowler would have been Peter Chapman right??'

'That's right....their big-headed star bowler. The one who had trials for the county - and don't we all know it!'

'You're not a fan of Peter Chapman yourself then Mr. Heath?'

'Arrogant, intimidating, big-headed, a wind-up merchant - and a bully! No, I'm not a fan of Peter Chapman. Not a fan at all...'

***

Davieson got back to his desk at *The Morning Chronicle* offices to write up his next instalment of the news story at hand. The return drive had been equally enjoyable and seemed to take no time at all as scenes of the historic accident continued to fill and flow through his head.

Back in the office, it was now time to craft a story from the various notes he had been making.

He threw his blazer jacket over the arms of his leather-backed chair, took his notepad out and set it beside a virgin sheet of paper. He was just about to put pen to paper when Justine Rose popped in. He looked up and smiled.

'Hello Justine'

'Hi, Merv. I answered your phone for you whilst you were out and took this brief message down. I - errr, didn't leave it on your desk as it sounded important, but I've been looking out for you and noticed you return just now'

The raven-headed beauty handed him a sheet from a message pad and studied his reaction inquisitively.

Davieson read the note:

Phone Chief Inspector Kent - Urgent

Justine could not gauge exactly how excited her colleague was with the news - he excelled at keeping his cards close to his chest, and he was very matter-of-fact in his response:

'Thank you, Justine'

Justine guessed, therefore, that she was no longer required, and quietly made her way back to her own desk and her own nostalgic story surrounding a local factory closure.

Davieson waited until she was out of earshot and then picked up his desk phone. His fingers shook slightly as he rapidly dialled a telephone number now firmly committed to memory.

The phone was promptly answered at the other end and the Welshman immediately asked to be put through to Chief Inspector Kent.

'I'm sorry sir. Chief Inspector Kent is currently out conducting interviews. Can another officer help?'

Davieson was sure they couldn't:

'I don't think so no'

'Well, can I take a message for him then?'

'Yes - that would be fine. Tell him Merv Davieson, of *The Morning Chronicle*, returned his call please'

'I will do sir - can I take a number?'

Davieson left his details and started with his story. He felt energised and tore joyously into the work at hand...

***

A more than decent update crafted (his editor would undoubtedly be pleased!) and Davieson decided to head home a little earlier than was normal to research a theory that was now playing on his mind.

En route he referenced the scorecard once again and decided to make one stop along the way.

He needn't have bothered - there was no answer.

Still - he could think as he drove, and the unorthodox route home did not delay him unduly. He would still have the remains of the afternoon, and all evening (until fatigue got the better of him), to thoroughly research his theory.

He got home, made a *rough-and-ready* plate of sandwiches - and poured himself a large single malt.

Decamping to his lounge, he reached up to his sturdy bookshelves and retrieved the largest volume housed there - a heavy, oversized (but quite beautiful) leather-bound copy of *The King James Bible*. It was a turn-of-the 20th century *Cambridge University Press* version that had been a family heirloom and had migrated with him from *South Wales*.

The Welshman grabbed his notepad, grabbed a biro - and began Bible study...

Chapter Nineteen

'Can we drive by any local sewage farms on the way back to *Police Headquarters* please Jones? I'm keen to get some fresh air down my lungs...what a sickening filthy mess!'

The Chief Inspector pulled a handkerchief out of his pocket and tried to wipe the sticky remnants of a half-sucked mint humbug from his fingers. He'd had the misfortune to accidentally pop his hand down the sides of the sofa he and Jones had sat on, whilst grilling Roger Lenton at the latter's property.

It was also a Saturday when Kent had originally planned to take some leave. He was consequently not in the best spirits, and Jones' drive back with his superior was likely to be a tense one.

'It was a pigsty alright sir. I don't think he gets out much do you?'

'No I don't. Pastiest pallor I've seen all summer...and with all this sunshine around too. It can't be healthy for the man!'

'No sir'

'There's something fishy about him too - and I don't mean the Boil in the Bag Kippers he's obviously devoured in the last day or too either'

Jones laughed at his Chief Inspector's sense of humour, but knew his superior was masking irritation and frustration.

'*Headquarters* then sir?'
'*Headquarters*, yes'
They drove off...

***

In his office at *Police Headquarters*, Kent had barely settled himself into the desk chair with a welcome mug of coffee when a call came through to his desk phone.

He grabbed the receiver instantly:
'Kent'
'Afternoon Chief Inspector. I've a Merv Davieson asking for you'
'About time too! Put him straight through please'
At that moment, the door burst open and a colleague bought a paper message with him into his office:
'Sorry to interrupt Chief Inspector. This chap asked you to call him when you returned to *Headquarters*'
He handed the Chief Inspector the note. The latter took it and read *Merv Davieson,* and his number, written upon it. He covered the mouthpiece of the telephone:
'Yes, thank you - I'm on it!'

The messenger retired. His superior looked irked, so he quietly shut the office door behind him and left the Chief Inspector to his call in peace.

There was a slight click on the phone as the call was transferred, and then Kent heard the familiar Welsh lilt:

'Afternoon Chief Inspector. I'm returning your call'

'Yes, thank you Davieson. I think you've something we require'

'Oh??'

'Yes - I believe you have the scorecard relating to the match in which Roger Lenton suffered his accident?'

'I have yes' confirmed the Welshman.

'I'm going to have to commandeer it I'm afraid'

'No problem Chief Inspector...I have all the details I might need for my story, and anyway - I have something else for you too'

'You do??'

'Yes - can we meet up, please? I can give it to you then'

'Sure. Where do you want to meet?'

'Fancy a pint?

Kent laughed:

'Well, why not. Know anywhere with a nice beer garden?'

'How about *The Mason's Arms, Upper Woodleigh*?'

'Perfect...'

***

Chief Inspector Kent paid for two beers and wandered outside to the beer garden where he found Davieson sunning himself at a picnic table. He set the pint glasses down and they both took a sip.

'The scorecard then Davieson!'

'Yes, of course - here it is'

The Welshman reached into his blazer pocket and produced the exhibit that had thus far eluded and frustrated Kent. He handed it to the tall policeman.

'And you've something else you said??'

'I have indeed. Yes, I've been thinking hard about the two parcels Chief Inspector'

'Oh??'

'Yes, I think I know what this is about'

'The cricket match yes, Davieson...I'm sure Roger Lenton is holding something back - and maybe Geoffrey Wright too!'

'You misunderstand me, no - I think I know what this is specifically about! Are you familiar with the *Volume of the Sacred Law* Chief Inspector?'

Chief Inspector Kent reddened and floundered. Davieson chipped in again:

'You could always book yourself into a local and reputable hotel. A chain hotel would be best - they're bound to have a copy of the *Gideon Bible* in the drawers of every room they have free'

'Well I guess so, but...'

'Relax Chief Inspector...I'm teasing you. Here you can use this'

Davieson handed the tall policeman a more manageable copy than the version he had perused intently the previous evening. Kent took it.

'Errr, thank you Davieson. It's a Bible...so what??'

'*The Greatest Story Ever Told* they say. Always has been...always will be. But I think there are four particular passages that I think will be of interest to you. I've put a scrap of paper in the relevant pages to help you - clearly annotated with the book, chapter and verse. Read them, and I think you'll see what I'm driving at'

'I appreciate that thank you'

'I, errr - also typed them all out fully and made you a copy. I was keen to gauge your opinion this minute, and see if you think I was on to anything'

Davieson handed Kent an A4 sheet of paper. The four passages were neatly spaced for ease of reading. Kent read them:

Exodus Chapter 21, verses 24 and 25
Eye for eye, tooth for tooth, hand for hand, foot for foot, Burning for burning, wound for wound, stripe for stripe.

Leviticus Chapter 24, verse 17
And he that killeth any man shall surely be put to death.

Deuteronomy Chapter 19, verses 19-21

Then shall ye do unto him, as he had thought to have done unto his brother: so shalt thou put the evil away from among you. And those which remain shall hear, and fear, and shall henceforth commit no more any such evil among you. And thine eye shall not pity; but life shall go for life, eye for eye, tooth for tooth, hand for hand, foot for foot.

Matthew Chapter 5, verse 38

Ye have heard that it hath been said, An eye for an eye, and a tooth for a tooth.

Kent's eyes twinkled in the way Davieson's often did when the latter's mind unravelled a problem at hand.

Davieson smiled at him:

'Geoffrey Wright received an eye right?'

'He did indeed'

'...And then a tooth?'

'He did too. Good work Davieson!'

'Thank you'

'...Hey - you don't think there's a severed hand caught up in the postal network do you and soon to be delivered to Geoffrey Wright?'

Davieson shrugged his shoulders but didn't answer.

'Well, I think it's time we spoke to Mr. Lenton again...and maybe Geoffrey Wright too'

'That may be so, but, in your enquiries to date, have you spoken to Peter Chapman as yet?- the bowler at hand when this awful accident occurred!'

The policeman shook his head:

'No, we've been working our way through the cricket club - but that's one individual we still need to catch up with'

Davieson nodded thoughtfully:

'He wasn't in when I called earlier. Given these ancient words of wisdom then...God's revealed will and word if you like. And given the fact that not only do these words follow the same *eye-tooth* sequence as you have on your hands here - but they also talk about retribution for whoever commits the first wrong, or inflicts the first harm done...then I think we should get there pronto...'

Chapter Twenty

'Care to jump in then?'

'I'd love to Chief Inspector'

Davieson was delighted to be offered the chance to arrive at Peter Chapman's abode as part of the official police presence...and not *just after* them. It was a privileged position to be in, and an opportunity not to be refused - even though the commute would be ridiculously short!

Their police car was being followed by another couple of support vehicles. He and Kent had managed to polish off an additional crafty half before the support Kent had ordered in, arrived and met them at *The Mason's Arms*.

As they set off, and the police driver made his way towards Peter Chapman's house, the Welshman started polite conversation:

'So you've seen Peter Chapman's place then Chief Inspector??'

'Not myself no. I sent various men out to try and speak to various people who might be connected with this affair. I couldn't conduct all the visits myself, you understand, but I've attended all the important ones...you know - the post office, Roger Lenton, and so on'

'The important ones, yes - I expect you needed to' mused Davieson, and then added:

'It's an impressive place'

'Is it?'

'Yes, it's a barn conversion you know?'

'Lovely'

'...Set back from the road'

'Nice'

'...Lovely rural location'

Kent turned to him, caught a little off-guard. Davieson seemed to be making an awful lot of conversation about the man's house...*maybe he was nervously excited and rambling a little. He was certainly smiling to himself.*

The Chief Inspector decided to stay silent for the remainder of the journey.

He wasn't silent for long, and in due time the driver turned the police car off *Rowley Hill Lane* and on to an all-too-familiar stretch of quiet country lane. Kent nearly leapt out of the back seat - his eyes nearly popped out of his head, as he grabbed and gripped Davieson's right arm more forcibly than was appropriate!:

'Here - that's the lay-by where we parked up when we searched the woods!'

The Welshman chuckled:

'It is indeed Chief Inspector'

At that very moment, the driver swung the car hard left, throwing the unprepared Chief Inspector to the right and clumsily into Davieson. He straightened himself up, embarrassed. They proceeded up Peter's Chapman's lengthy driveway, past an ornate double-garage, to his smart and impressive barn conversion - and parked up.

Kent's mouth was still wide open. He slobbered slightly!

'Well we're here Chief Inspector'

Kent jumped out of the car and stared back down the driveway. He could clearly see the lay-by from the house. Similarly - cars parked in the lay-by could clearly see Peter Chapman's property'

'This proximity has to be significant Davieson'

The journalist shrugged his shoulders:

'Maybe Chief Inspector...maybe'

'Right!...let's look him up'

A total of seven of them walked up to the front door of Peter Chapman's home, and Kent rang the doorbell.

He gave it a minute and then rapped the door hard instead.

There was no answer. He tried a second time, but still no answer or noise inside. He knocked a third and final time for good order - and then nodded at one of his men:

'Break it down please'

The man addressed nodded and went about his business in a calm and collected way. In no time at all the door was open and Kent stepped inside to lead the way.

The first thing that hit them was the stench! Each man screwed his face up, reverted to breathing through their' mouths, and reached for his own handkerchief to shield his nostrils from the offensive odour - Kent inadvertently smearing sticky humbug across the bridge of his nose. He cursed!

The professionals amongst them knew when to expect a corpse...and Davieson had a good idea of what they would find too - especially when two or three large bluebottles flew their way, and on towards the freedom of the forced-open front door.

The others followed Kent, passing a pale green summer jacket hung on a coat stand. A bunch of house keys - and car keys, lay in a small bowl near to the front door.

They edged slowly down the hallway, following the Chief Inspector.

They found him in the kitchen. Lying on his back, a small pool of congealed blood on the lino flooring beside him - and three stab wounds as they had seen on the other bodies! There were two larger pools of blood around his head and mouth area.

Kent edged cautiously closer to take a better look, and the others followed.

A bloodied and empty eye socket drew everyone's breath. The remaining eye was still open...and then they noticed the mouth. It was gaping wide open and blood had spilt and trickled from the corner, onto the floor. A bluebottle suddenly flew out of it and repulsed all of them, causing them to back away. It was a disgusting sight, even for the experienced professional!

Davieson thought Sergeant Jones looked like he might throw up, and was thankful that he himself did not appear to be as fazed by their find!

'Nobody touch anything!'

Davieson felt the Chief Inspector's command was largely given for his own benefit, so he took it upon himself to answer for all:

'Of course Chief Inspector'

Thinking that he might be ushered out of the room at any moment, once Kent had locked the crime scene fully down, the Welshman quickly scanned the room for anything of interest.

He noted that on the otherwise-empty kitchen table were tins of dog food *and was that a hint of a muddy boot print on the kitchen floor??* There were a few washing up pots on the draining board next to the sink, but little by way of a *scene* as such (or clue), as to what exactly had taken place here earlier.

'I want a thorough search of this property - and the grounds Jones, for any clue that may shed light on what's happened here...and why'

'Righto sir'

'Catalogue everything if you have to!'

'Will do sir'

'And get everything taped off - this room, the front door, the entrance to the drive...the lot!'

'I'll get straight on to that now sir'

'And I want this man's final movements clearly understood. I want to know when everyone who knew him saw him last....and the circumstances. I want anyone who didn't know him - but might have seen him, to fill the detail in too. Get his mugshot out there and all over the place!'

With Kent continuing to issue orders and take command of proceedings, Davieson casually wandered out of the kitchen and into a lounge area. He ran his journalistic eyes around the room for anything that may help him with the background, for another exciting newspaper article that he would soon be crafting.

The room was dominated by a large (self-indulgent) canvas print, showing Peter Chapman in whites, charging in to bowl. The photographer had managed to capture the action, just as he had released the ball. It was a terrific piece of sports photography, and the Welshman could quite understand why the deceased had obviously been fond of it too, and allowed it to take pride of place within his lovely home.

He bent over to a framed photograph on a bookshelf, and lowered his oval spectacles to peer over them and focus correctly. The photograph was of a man in a coat, with his faithful dog at his heels. The man was certainly the man they had just found slain in his kitchen! He turned his head:

'Chief Inspector!'

The tall policeman's face appeared at the door and he hurried over, once he had located his friend:

'What is it?'

'We've, errr - found our *Yorky* friend!'

Kent stooped down to take a look alongside the Welshman himself (who was still doing the same), but his long gangly legs made his posture somewhat more exaggerated and comically awkward.

'I think you're right, yes'

'...And that appears to be Peter Chapman!'

'It does indeed Davieson'

The latter nodded. He stood up, straightened his back and look at the detective:

'So, Peter Chapman's dog...and not that of the body in the woods then??'

'Hmm' was all Kent could reply...

***

Davieson and Kent strolled back to their cars. Both of them blew hard enough for their cheeks to swell. Viewing a crime scene was never a pleasant affair when murder and blood were involved. You were viewing something that was fundamentally wrong, but you were also already too late to prevent it or influence a better outcome.

And this viewing had been particularly gruesome!

The Chief Inspector spoke first:

'Well the case progresses at a pace at last, and the more I now pause to reflect on things...the more I think that there's something *fishy* about Roger Lenton. I don't like the way he doesn't give you eye contact when you speak to the man, so I'm sure that he's holding something back from us, and is involved in matters here right up to his neck!'

Davieson nodded silently:

'You don't like the way he looks at you, you say??'

'No I don't!'

'Well, it is a glass eye Chief Inspector....'

Chapter Twenty-One

In the offices of *The Morning Chronicle*, Davieson was furiously writing up *BOWLER BUTCHERED!*

He had ditched the light grey sports blazer over the back of his seat, and his green tie had been slackened off to an overly-generous extent - now hanging loosely from his neck, and resting nowhere near his *Adam's Apple*. He was comfortable - and could now concentrate without any distracting resistance upon his person.

He pretty much had the whole story mapped out in his head...now his readers needed a usable version presented to them.

Sometimes a clever - and quite, quite sophisticated headline was essentially what was required...other times you simply needed to shock your readership, and help sell newspapers!

Kent had allowed him to use the photograph of Peter Chapman and his dog, that he had found in the lounge, to accompany his story.

He was starting to hone his first draft when Justine Rose breezed past. She was wearing a bright red number, and the vibrant colour caught the Welshman's attention out of the corner of his eye.

'Justine!'

She pirouetted on the spot, the change in direction shaking her lovely long black hair:

'Hi Merv'

'You've got a dog right??'

She looked confused:

'Errr - yeah'

'Big or small?'

'Small - it's a *Jack Russell*'

'Ok - and how many tins of dog food do you get through please?'

'Big tins or small tins Merv?'

He worked his thumbs and fingers up either side of a chin and jaw sporting three days worth of beard growth, in concerted consideration:

'Errr, the big tins I guess, you know - a tin of baked beans-sized'

'Oh, one of those a day. I get two meals out of it, so I serve half in the morning - and save half to serve up later'

'Before or after walking the dog?'

'Oh always after Merv. We go for a walk - work a good appetite up...then reward afterwards. Let it all drop whilst you're at work - and then the same pattern again later. It's what they say is best...and Charlie agrees too'

'Your partner??'

'My *Jack Russell* Merv!!'

'Oh...sorry!'

He looked genuinely embarrassed...Justine, on the other hand, looked mildly vexed!

She forgave him the slip:

'Anyway, are you looking into getting one??'

He pushed the frame of his spectacles back into position on the bridge of his nose - the spectacles had started to work their way down his nose as he worked busily on his story.

'I'm looking into something Justine...'

***

Sergeant Simpkins parked up, put on the best *poker face* he could muster, exhaled - and rapped the front door of the house where the parents of Rebecca Chapman resided.

An elderly man opened the door. He looked disturbed when he noticed the police uniform:

'Hello' he said warily.

'Hello, sir. Is Rebecca Chapman in please?'

The elderly man gently nodded:

'You better come in'

'Thank you, sir'

Simpkins followed the man through to a sitting room, An elderly lady was sat in an armchair. *His wife and Rebecca's mother Simpkins assumed.*

The man stood at the foot of the stairs, his hand on the banister post to steady himself - and called upstairs:

'Rebecca! There a policeman asking for you'

Simpkins heard footsteps descending, and a younger lady entered the sitting room:

'Hello. Is something wrong??'

Simpkins pointed to the sofa:

'Take a seat please madam'

Rebecca Chapman sat down, shooting a quick glance left-right at her parents...they both shrugged at her. She looked back at Sergeant Simpkins:

'What's this about please?'

'I'm afraid, Mrs. Chapman, that we've found a body!'

She put her hands up to her mouth, and her eyes widened somewhat:

'A body??'

'Yes madam'

Frown lines appeared across her forehead:

'Yes - but I thought that was a few days ago?? I read it in the newspaper in fact, so I don't understand why you're telling me that now??'

Simpkins slowly blinked and nodded, sympathetic to her confusion:

'Ah, well we've found another body I'm afraid madam. We, errr - believe it to be that of your husband, Peter Chapman!'

'Peter??'

She looked shocked. She stood up and turned her back on Simpkins.

Was that why he didn't answer his door??

'I'm sorry to be the bringer of bad news Mrs. Chapman' the sergeant apologised: 'But I'm here to ask if you can accompany me, and formally identify the body for us please?'

Rebecca huffed in disgust, she spun around. Her manner had changed in an instant:

'Well he's nothing to do with me now!' she snapped.

Simpkins threw an exaggerated baffled look, and theatrically referred to his notepad:

'Well according to our records, he is your husband - is he not, Mrs. Chapman??'

'Well technically yes, legally yes - but we're separated, and that's why I'm living here with my parents'

She was getting angrier by the minute.

'...Well, it shouldn't take long Mrs. Chapman...purely routine...'

'He's done nothing for me of late...and I'm not prepared to do this for him I'm afraid! You better ask his brother'

The elderly man stood up and addressed Simpkins:

'I think you better leave!'

He showed Simpkins out.

The sergeant headed back to his car - his tail between his legs.

He shook his head.

He shouldn't have let himself be rolled over as easily as that - he was always no good in these emotive situations. Chief Inspector Kent would not be best pleased with him. He was certain of that...

Chapter Twenty-Two

Craig Ellsmere was in his kitchen. The coffee was already made, and out popped two slices of toast from the toaster, right on cue. He buttered them liberally on a side plate, and then carried both mug of coffee - and the plate of toast, to the kitchen table.

The letterbox rattled, so he quickly nipped along the hallway to collect his morning newspaper before sitting down. Breakfast preparations all complete, he took a munch of toast, sat down...and unrolled *The Sunday Chronicle*.

He immediately slowed his chewing to something sloth-like - his eyes widening and nearly popping out of his head in disbelief, as he saw the cricket club...and Peter Chapman, splashed all over the front page.

He quickly got himself acquainted with the details...and then read it all again to make sure he wasn't dreaming or mistaken.

He wasn't mistaken alright!
'Well well well'
He shook his head and yelled his wife:

'Come and look at this dear...you'll never believe it!'

Mrs. Ellsmere entered the kitchen in her dressing gown and Craig Ellsmere handed his wife the paper. She read the front page and put it vacantly down on the kitchen table.

She looked physically shocked and put her hand to her mouth:

'I don't know what to say, dear'

'No....Still - an opportunity for our other bowlers (and the young lad in particular) to tighten things up, and for our batsmen maybe to forge more commanding leads!'

'Oh Craig - that's an awful thing to say!'

Mrs. Ellsmere looked disapprovingly at her husband. Craig Ellsmere simply grinned...

***

Tucked tightly under his arm, Ted Ellis took his copy of *The Sunday Chronicle* out on to the pavilion terrace, with a steaming mug of tea that Bob had just made for him. Not too milky, and no sugar - just how he liked it.

He still could not quite believe that their own village - and the cricket club for that matter, had managed to make the front pages of the National newspapers.

He set the mug down on the terrace deck, unfolded the paper - and read the bold headline emblazoned across the front page once again:

BOWLER BUTCHERED!

No wonder he hadn't featured in the last match. He had thought his absence strange...given his talent and obvious talismanic (if often unpopular) qualities.

He eagerly flicked the page over to get the finer details of the story - reported by a Merv Davieson, that began on page two.

He read in horror the details of the fatal wounds and mutilation that their own Peter Chapman had suffered. He frowned as he read of the curious sharp, uniform, wounds.

Ted Ellis abandoned his tea and took the paper back inside the pavilion.

He found Bob Butler in the bar, where he expected him to be:

'Here, have you read this Bob?'

The barman looked up from polishing the bar top with a dry beer towel:

'I, errr - could hardly miss it, Ted. I've got a copy there'

He nodded towards another copy of *The Sunday Chronicle* lying on the end of the bar.

'What do you think about the way he was killed?'

'Horrible!'

'You errr - don't think it had anything to do with my equipment that went missing do you??...I never did find it'

'I really don't know Ted'

'Well, do you think I should say something?'

Bob Butler stopped what he was doing:

'I don't know Ted, But if it's bothering you - I should tell the police and let them decide if it's important or not'

Ted looked back down at his newspaper:

'I think you're right Bob...thank you. It says here that a Chief Inspector Kent is heading the investigation...'

***

'Glad you had a lovely stay - and we hope to see you again sometime soon'

'It's been lovely thanks. Bye bye'

Having checked out of their room at *The Grand Hotel*, the elderly couple picked up their suitcases and departed through the revolving door onto a seafront bathed in sunshine. They were part of a package coach holiday, and were in good time to make their scheduled pick-up on the promenade.

The lobby was once again deserted, so the receptionist took the opportunity to keep herself abreast of anything newsworthy. She'd temporarily borrowed the hotel's copy of *The Sunday Chronicle*, from the selection of *dailies* the hotel kept in the lobby for their residents' perusal.

She read the headline...she looked at the accompanying photograph of a man with his dog.

Surely this man was staying here??

She brought the newspaper up close to her eyes, to get a more detailed look at him.

She was certain. She knew it!

The receptionist picked the newspaper up, briefly abandoned the reception desk - and quickly sought out the General Manager.

'Have you seen this story, sir?'

'You can hardly miss it!'

She held the paper up and pointed at the photograph. She tapped it twice with her fingers to indicate it further:

'This chap was staying here sir...and it sounds like staying here just before all of this happened!'

The General Manager put down the paperwork he had been dealing with:

'Are you sure?'

'Positive sir'

'Let me see the guest book please'

The General Manager followed her back through to the lobby. It was still thankfully deserted. She opened the guest book up, and ran her fingers back to the Friday in question - mentally remembering faces against the various names of guests detailed before her.

Some brought back fond memories...others not so. She stopped her finger:

'That's him. Peter Smith....Mr. & Mrs. Peter Smith!'

The General Manager re-read the front page of *The Sunday Chronicle*:

'It says here, that this gentleman was a *Peter Chapman*'

'It's definitely him sir!'

'You're positive??'

'Absolutely. And there's another thing...'

'What??'

'Mrs. Smith wasn't wearing a wedding ring...neither of them was in fact'

'A secretive dirty weekend??' suggested the General Manager.

'Probably'

They managed a faint smile.

'Well, we better phone the police then!'

***

A noxious odour wafted along the corridors of *Police Headquarters*.

Chief Inspector Kent had pulled Roger Lenton in for questioning, and had kept him detained in a suitable interview room.

They had also taken the opportunity to remove a copy of a Bible from his home when they collected him - by far the cleanest item they had managed to identify, within premises that Kent would not have kept a pig in!

The door to the interview room was firmly shut - with Roger Lenton sat inside, but still, traces of his recent whereabouts lingered unpleasantly from the reception front desk, into the bowels of *Headquarters*.

Kent burst into the interview room with Sergeant Jones - immediately screwing his face up somewhat, and startling Roger Lenton.

The Chief Inspector sat down and folded his arms. He looked full of confidence and extremely sure of himself:

'I'm sure you're aware sir, that we have found Peter Chapman!'

Roger Lenton looked blankly back at him.

'Where has he been?'

'What do you mean where has he been?'

'Has he been away?? I'm sorry, I didn't know that he was missing!'

'Are you trying to be funny with us sir?'

Roger Lenton frowned:

I'm sorry - I'm not following...'

'Oh come on man - it's all over the papers'

'I'm afraid I don't read them'

'No problem sir - I've got a copy here, you can have mine!'

The tall detective virtually threw his copy of *The Sunday Chronicle* at his interviewee. The eye-catching headline could not fail to be missed, but there was no reaction or response, so Kent continued:

'Someone had taken his eye out sir!'

'Well that sounds terrible I suppose...'

He still looked or appeared confused.

'Peter Chapman took *your* eye out, didn't he sir?'

'Well, kind of...I guess' muttered the former wicket-keeper of *Upper Woodleigh Cricket Club*.

'It's an awful coincidence...wouldn't you say sir??...'

Chapter Twenty-Three

Davieson decided that he would work from home, and *in the field*, that Monday morning. His editor was extremely pleased with the sensationalist story, and agreed that he could pursue its further developments as best he saw fit.

He first phoned *Police Headquarters* and asked for Kent.

'Chief Inspector!'

'Morning Davieson...good piece yesterday by the way'

'Thank you, Chief Inspector'

'Anyway - what can I do for you?'

'I was wondering if you were nearer to establishing what exactly had transpired at Peter Chapman's place, prior to us finding him?'

'Well some of the detail is starting to fall into place yes'

'Such as??'

'Well, it looks like Peter Chapman arrived home at his barn conversion, parked his expensive motor in his double garage, locked the garage - and let himself into the house.

He appears to have been peckish and made himself a cheese sandwich - washed down with a glass of water.

He would then appear to have been brutally murdered, sometime later, by the same unknown assailant responsible for the murder in the woods (murders I guess!) - given that it was the same weapon used.

We also believe that he knew this assailant, and let the killer into his house, as there was no sign of a break in or struggle'

Davieson was making shorthand notes.

'I noticed a boot print Chief Inspector'

'You did, did you? You're sharp Davieson - I'll give you that. Yes, there was a size eleven *Wellington* boot print on the kitchen floor. It is *not* that of Peter Chapman, and we suspect likely muddied in the woods - probably when burying the other chap and the dog, as it doesn't belong to that body either!'

The Welshman was silent.

'Hello??'

'Still here Chief Inspector...just making notes. So you think there's something in this *Wellington* boot print then and equally that the woods man hadn't murdered Peter Chapman first then?'

'We do Davieson - we do indeed'

'And have you checked Peter Chapman's stomach contents Chief Inspector?'

'His *stomach contents*??'

'Yes'

'We haven't, no'

'Well, I'd recommend that you have your forensic pathologist do that pronto for good order Chief Inspector!'

'You do??'

'I do...just a hunch of mine. Let me know how that goes please'

The Welshman hung up...

***

The postman rattled the letterbox. Alan Chambers heard his jolly whistle gradually fade, as the postman walked back down his drive, and continued on his rounds.

The secretary of *Upper Woodleigh Cricket Club* took his mug of tea with him and wandered through to the hall from his kitchen. He stooped down briefly to retrieve an envelope from the letterbox and headed back to his kitchen.

He set the tea down on the table and was just about to open the envelope as two rounds of bread popped out of the toaster.

He dealt with the toast whilst they were warm, spreading them with butter, and took a small side plate back to the kitchen table.

He opened the letter and read:

You are summoned to attend an extraordinary committee meeting of Upper Woodleigh Cricket Club.

To be held at the Pavilion, at 6.00 p.m. prompt.

On Wednesday 24th July.

Agenda:
1) How are we to restore the fine name of U.W.C.C?
2) How do we eradicate the memory of Peter Chapman from our records?

Your Chairman
John

It was signed by John Middleton.

Short notice - short (concise) agenda...and it's obviously preying on John's mind if he's sent this out direct, thought Alan. *Cricket Club correspondence would normally be circulated by me as club Secretary. Maybe there just isn't time, and it can't wait?*

He checked his calendar. He had nothing on. Good job he guessed - this sounded serious...

***

He wondered if the girl would have remembered anything as yet, as he drove out to *Folestree Parva*, straight after the call with Kent. He knew that she would be running the operation today.

Having arrived in the village, he headed for the post office. It was a quiet day, but he was unable to park immediately in front of the post office, as a result of a blue vehicle parked illegally and half on double-yellow lines.

Wasn't that there last time I was here?

He parked further down the road, got out - and walked back along the pavement in the direction of the post office.

As he passed the blue vehicle, he looked curiously at the windscreen and found that there were three parking tickets affixed to it. The driver couldn't safely drive the car away without removing them, as collectively they probably blocked out about three-quarters of the visible road ahead. He shook his head and headed inside.

The post office was empty...save for Mandy behind the counter. He had expected to see the gentleman inside, who was being served last time he drove out here - the blue car man, but *no - now he thought of it the blue car was still there last time he left...it couldn't have been his.*

He smiled at Mandy and unfolded the copy of *The Sunday Chronicle* carrying the striking *BOWLER*

BUTCHERED! headline. He placed it on the counter where she could see it clearly:

'Hello, Mandy. The police now know from whom the *parts* were taken that were posted here then!'

She looked disgusted:

'I heard that yes, and it's even worse now there's a name behind it...you start to really feel for the man, now he has an identity and isn't an unidentified entity you know??'

'I can well imagine...I'm sorry'

'I can barely concentrate on my work here'

'No I guess not. I'd, errr - wondered if the progress the police are now making had stimulated any further recollections as yet, as to who had handed the printed label parcels in for posting??'

She shook her head:

'It hasn't I'm afraid. I can remember my holiday break in *Bathcombe Bay*...that was lovely, and lots of good memories still fresh there - but I can't for the life of me remember that day in the post office in any detail'

'Maybe because holidays are a break from the mundane??...they tend to stand out and be fondly memorable' suggested Davieson.

She nodded:

'I'm sure you're right - and I wasn't trying to be unhelpful for the police...that's just not like me'

'I'm sure it's not Mandy' he reassured her:
'*Bathcombe Bay* eh??' he added absently.

'...Have you been there?'

'Oh yes...a few years ago now though, but I enjoyed my time there'

Davieson briefly weighed up the merits of elaborating, and explaining that it was there where he had made quite a name for himself - but he decided against it...*it was vain, and she was probably too young to have remembered the story in any detail anyway.*

She smiled:

'Yes - it's a really pretty seafront there'

'Anyway - that car outside...the postmaster's??'

'A pain isn't it?'

'Sure is...it's scuppered my intended parking twice now!...So is it?'

'No, it's not his - he's not the culprit. We don't know whose it is I'm afraid. The postmaster formally complained but all he got was this...'

She grabbed a formal looking letter - which at first glance, appeared to Davieson to be headed with the logo of *Haverton Borough Council*. She read aloud verbatim from the closing paragraph:

'In order to be classified as abandoned the vehicle also needs to be untaxed for at least one month and left in the same location for a significant amount of time.

...So we're unsure exactly if we're to suffer it sat there for a few more weeks yet - or whether they will eventually tow it away!'

'Council red tape eh!' joked Davieson: 'Well, let me know if you recall anything please'

'Will do'

He bade her farewell...

Chapter Twenty-Four

The police cars drove in convoy along the promenade at *Bathcombe Bay*.

The promenade itself was busy and full of pedestrian holidaymakers and day-trippers...many carrying ice creams, enjoying another pleasant and cloudless day at the coast.

'This is the place. Park up here please!'

'Righto Chief Inspector'

One by one, Kent and his entourage filed through the revolving doors of the most salubrious seafront hotel in *Bathcombe Bay - The Grand Hotel*. They were four-strong.

The General Manager had arranged cover and ensured that both he, and the receptionist, were relieved of immediate duties, whilst they helped and assisted the police with their enquiries. The clientele of *The Grand* would not be inconvenienced - despite the turn of events, and the hotel's part it had played in the last known movements of a murdered man!

They were shown into the small office immediately behind the reception desk. There were just three seats in there, and that meant standing room only for three of them! Kent quickly commandeered one of the seats and suggested the General Manager and the receptionist took the other two.

The receptionist looked apprehensive - intimidated by a larger police presence than she had envisaged. The General Manager looked calm.

'Now, when did he check in please sir?'

'Mr. Smith checked in here on the Friday...Friday the 5th'

'Mr. Chapman, you mean??'

'Yes I'm sorry - Mr. Chapman'

'And he checked in as part of a couple?'

'That's right. Yes - he checked into a double en-suite room with Mrs....errr, *Smith*!'

'And when did they check out please?'

'Late morning on the Sunday...the 7th'

'Thank you. And what did Mrs....*Smith*, look like, please? Can either or both of you provide a detailed description??'

Kent shot them both a glance, back and forth.

The receptionist chipped in:

'Well she was quite tall for a lady'

'How tall would you guess?'

'I dunno...5 feet 8 *maybe*??'

'Ok. Carry on please'

'I'd say that she was younger than him...'

'Age??'

'I dunno...young twenties I would have thought'

'Hair colour?'
'Dark'
'Hairstyle??'
'A short bob'

Kent checked that Sergeant Jones, who was stood just to his left and hovering over his shoulders, was noting all of this down.

'Eye colour??'
'Brown I think...I'm not too sure'
'And do you remember what was she wearing?'
'She looked very summery'
'Summery??'
'Yes. Nice blue summer dress, white cardigan, a red ladies neckerchief - with large white polka dots upon it, and a red beret'
'Shoes??'
'I can't really see our customers' shoes - stationed behind the reception desk I mean...sorry'
'Nevermind, that's a good description to be going on with – a few more facial questions in a while to help us further, but who signed in here? Him? Her?...Or both of them?'
'Just him Chief Inspector'
'Do you mind fetching me the guest book please?'

The General Manger stood up:

'Not at all. I'll fetch that for you now'

He retrieved the guest book from reception and handed it to the tall policeman.

'Thank you, sir'

He perused the page and date in question, produced a handwritten note from his pocket, entombed within a clear evidence bag - and compared the handwriting. He nodded, satisfied - and looked at one of his men:

'Peter Chapman...Peter Smith - it was him all right staying here! We may need to keep this at some point - but can we photograph the cover and this page for now please?'

'Righto sir'

Kent addressed the receptionist:

'So, do you think you would recognise this young lady if you were to see her again?'

She nodded:

'I think so, yes'

'Good'

The Chief Inspector smiled, stood up - his height dominating the small party assembled in the office, and looked down at both the General Manager and receptionist:

'Finally...did they seem to have been a couple for some time - or in the early stages of their, errr...relationship??'

The pair of them shrugged their shoulders and looked a little blankly at each other.

There was a moment of silence, that gradually grew a little uncomfortable as Kent continued to peer down at them, without response.

It was ended by the vintage phone on the reception desk ringing out and vibrating against the highly polished mahogany surface.

'Excuse me...'

The General Manager walked over and lifted the receiver:

'*The Grand Hotel - Bathcombe Bay...*'

He nodded his head, as he listened to the caller at the other end, then lowered the receiver and muffled the mouthpiece with his hand. He looked at Kent:

'Chief Inspector!...It's for you'

The tall policeman strolled over to the General Manager and grabbed the phone:

'Hello....'

'I've a Merv Davieson asking for you sir. Say's he's got a suggestion for you??'

'Put him through'

The phone clicked and the Welshman was put through by the call handler at *Police Headquarters*:

'Chief Inspector'

'Hello Davieson'

'You're at *Bathcombe Bay?*'

'We are indeed'

'I assume, it's still delightful??'

'Errr, I suppose so yes. I've barely had chance to take the place in though mind - we're on business here'

'Oh??'

'Not now Davieson. I'll give you a statement and update later though - I promise. In fact - I think you could be most helpful in helping us locate somebody, as quickly as possible'

'Well I look forward to helping you later then Chief Inspector - just let me know how I can help'

'Anyway...you've a suggestion for me I hear??'

'I have...please don't think me impertinent though - I appreciate I'm the amateur here'

'Not at all Davieson - I know you're an asset...I'm all ears??'

'I've a car registration for you, that I believe you should trace'

'Oh yeah?'

'Yes Chief Inspector. It's been parked up for some time outside the post office in *Folestree Parva*, where the parcels were posted. It's been parked there both of the times I've been out there covering the story - and it's now plastered in parking tickets. Nobody seems to be claiming it or moving it Chief Inspector!'

'The registration please?'

Kent took down the details...

Chapter Twenty-Five

Kent stepped out of *The Grand Hotel*, and onto a promenade at *Bathcombe Bay* that was bathed in sunshine.

A naturally dour man, the sound of waves gently breaking on the sandy shore, the sound of gulls screeching overhead - and the sound of a nostalgic barrel organ entertaining holidaymakers on the seafront, could not fail to lift his spirits.

...That and the case progressing, with a couple of good new leads for his men to follow up!

He clapped his hands together triumphantly and with intent:

'Something to go on Jones. Let's find this young lady pronto...we've got a promising description after all, and then look into Davieson's parked car'

A seagull flying overhead, chose just that very moment to *make itself comfortable* mid-flight.

Kent inclined his head to the left in trepidation and found he'd an unpleasantly-splattered shoulder.

His spirits promptly fell again:

'Tissue please Jones!'

***

Davieson was writing up *WHO WAS THE MYSTERY GIRL?*

Kent had kindly supplied him with a photograph of *The Grand Hotel*'s guest book, and a photo-fit of the girl the police were anxious to identify and locate.

His editor had agreed another day's front cover headline, for the chief crime reporter on his staff...and this pleased the Welshman enormously! He would do the piece justice, and hopefully get the nation looking out for - and helping identify, Peter Chapman's mystery lady.

He had almost finished the story when the phone on his desk rang. He penned the final full stop, put his pen down on the desk - and answered it:

'Davieson'

'Hello Chief Inspector'

'I thought I'd let you know that we've managed to trace the owner of that blue car parked up in *Folestree Parva*'

The Welshman grabbed his pen again:

'Go on'

'It's interesting all right - the owner was certainly not a local, so very odd to be parked up in *Folestree Parva* for so long. Equally, he was from nowhere surrounding the other locations these events have taken place in to date, either...'

'So who was the owner Chief Inspector?' pressed Davieson.

'One Richard Chapman. We don't know too much about the fellow, as of yet. But we have established one thing...he had a brother!'

'Peter Chapman' blurted Davieson down the phone.

'Peter Chapman indeed Davieson, so heartfelt thanks from myself and my men for the invaluable lead'

'My pleasure Chief Inspector'

'We're now matching the bloods of the two dead men as we speak. I'm thinking, you see, that the reason Richard Chapman could *not* retrieve his illegally-parked vehicle from outside of the post office...was that somebody (as yet unknown) had buried him by then in *Rowley Woods*!...'

Chapter Twenty-Six

The following morning, Jodi Fletcher strolled down the street, contemplating popping in somewhere to grab a takeaway coffee.

A middle-aged lady walking a dog was heading her way in the opposite direction. Jodi stepped to the side of the pavement, in order to give the dog (and its leash) sufficient room to pass. She addressed the lady as the three of them met and smiled politely at her:

'Morning'

'Errr Morning'

The friendliness was not reciprocated. The lady gave Jodi Fletcher a curious stare.

Oddball, thought Jodi, shook her head - and carried on. The coffee shop was just ahead now.

An elderly man was walking towards her, with his head buried in his newspaper. He heard her approaching footsteps and popped his head up to avoid colliding into her.

He gave her a funny look, looked up at her hat - then looked back at his newspaper...and continued to look at her, without blinking an eye, as he walked on by.

Was he staring at my beret??

She looked back over her shoulder and found the elderly man doing exactly the same thing. It gave her the creeps!

Have I got bird poo on my hat? Or mascara on my face?? Or maybe lipstick on my teeth???

Jodi Fletcher bounced paranoid possibilities around in her head. She popped into the coffee shop...*she'd check herself in the mirror in their toilets, and sort out whatever it was that was gaining her unwanted attention.*

She first ordered a takeaway latte, and paid for it at the counter:

'May I use the loo whilst I wait for it please?'

'Sure - it's just there. I'll leave the latte on the counter top here'

'Thank you'

She headed into the ladies - and ignoring the cubicles, made straight for a mirror above a sink unit. She gazed at her own reflection.

Nothing obvious!

She leant closer and inspected her face, hair and hat closely.

Still nothing.

She shook her head for the second time in as many minutes, left the ladies - and collected her latte.

Back on the street, she passed a newsagents and headed in to buy her copy of *The Morning Chronicle*.

She picked one up from a pile on the counter and smiled at the proprietor. He was of Indian origin and was tapping away quietly to himself as Asiatic music sounded from some music player hidden somewhere out of sight.

She produced coins from her purse and paid for the paper, thankful the newsagent paid her little attention and did not stare as others had done that morning.

She collected her change, stepped back out on to the pavement - and held her newspaper up.

And then she saw herself...*well a photo-fit of herself anyway* - but unmistakably her, on the front page of a national newspaper!

***

It was just Kent and Simpkins on this return.

Kent had set Sergeant Jones upon the task of continuing to collect sample footwear from each and every member of *Upper Woodleigh Cricket Club*...and the club's wider family!

The hapless sergeant was already working his way through the villagers of localised and connected interest, and would likely be tied up trying to achieve this for a full day or more.

Whilst part of the same wider line of enquiry, Kent wanted to handle this particular visit into town himself. It both showed his personal commitment to the task at hand, which would be noted by Jones and his other men in the field - and as far as he was concerned, he found the target a person of significant interest!

Simpkins parked up. They weaved their way clinically through the crowd of morning shoppers and once again entered the offices of *Latchford & Co.*

The timid receptionist never stood a chance again, as the two plain clothed policemen stepped through the door and waltzed straight through reception. She did half-rise out of her chair, only for the taller of the two to raise his palm in protestation:

'Don't worry madam...we know where we're going!'

She promptly sat back down and watched them ascend the flight of stairs that led to the first floor.

Kent found the Chief Accountant's office door closed.

He gave a cursory *knock knock* on the door, and immediately (and forcefully) opened it without any chance of his knock being acknowledged, or answered.

Geoffrey Wright gave a start.

'Morning Mr. Wright'

'Erm...morning'

'Would you mind taking off one of your shoes please?'

'My *what??*'

'Your shoes please sir'

He sighed - feeling somewhat cornered, and looked frustrated.

'May I ask why?'

'You can *ask*...' replied Kent sarcastically and leaving his reply hanging in the air. *He didn't elaborate or offer anything else further.*

'Left or right?'

'You decide sir'

'Well, errr...'

'...Your left shoe will be fine sir!'

'Very well!'

Geoffrey Wright was not a happy man...he was most definitely annoyed! He would have liked to have carried off an air of defiance (he thought he knew his rights)...but as it was, the hard-stare Chief Inspector Kent subjected him to, eroded his steely resolve - and he wisely defaulted to ready compliance.

He stooped down and removed the black patent leather formal slip-on shoe from his left foot.

Kent had advanced across the office - whilst he was bent there seeing to this and pounced immediately upon him as he stood back up:

'Pop it in there please sir'

Geoffrey Wright furrowed his brows and dropped his shoe into the clear plastic bag that the Chief Inspector had presented to him.

The latter peered inside...noted that it was a size eleven shoe - and thrust the bag under the nose of Sergeant Simpkins without speaking.

Simpkins looked into the bag, nodded - and Kent addressed the accountant:

'Sign this receipt here, please. We'll try and return it when we can'

'But...'

'Good day sir'

They left...

***

'Chief Inspector'

Kent looked up. His sergeant had answered the phone...*he normally did*:

'What is it Simpkins?'

'That journalist asking for you sir'

'Davieson??...I'll take it thanks'

He wrestled the phone off Simpkins, a little too quickly - briefly entwining the pair of them intimately together. Simpkins wormed himself noiselessly out of the muddle and brought an end to the embarrassment. His superior was blushing.

'Davieson - what can I do for you?'

'A quick question, if I may be so bold Chief Inspector??'

The southern-Welsh dulcet tones were hard to refuse...especially to one so useful to the cause, and he always asked so politely:

'I'm all ears...'

'You kindly gave me the description as to what Mrs., errr - *Smith* was wearing. I got it on our front page...as you've no doubt read'

'I have indeed Davieson - a good article! I'm sure it will reap rewards...but what of it?? - I thought you were going to ask me about the results of the blood analysis we conducted!'

'Ah yes. The bloods - was the other corpse that of Richard Chapman?'

'It was indeed - I don't know now if there's some kind of feuding families angle we should be considering here Davieson!'

'Well in that case, I'd start with all the Montagues in the locality Chief Inspector...and then move on to the Capulets. You could do with getting your hands on a phone book for starters'

'A phone book??'

Davieson's eyes twinkled mischievously.

'Nevermind Chief Inspector. Anyway, that wasn't what I was going to ask you'

'No??'

'No. You didn't tell me what Peter *Chapman-Smith* was wearing on his seaside vacation'

'*Peter Chapman??* Well we didn't ask Davieson - we'd found him you see...you were there when we did find him in fact. No, it was his lady friend we are after'

'Nevermind. Sorry to trouble you Chief Inspector'

The Welshman hung up...

***

An strange noise resonated around the reception void, as somebody started to descend the stairs rather awkwardly and head down from the first floor.

'Are you limping Geoff?'

The Chief Accountant paused halfway down. His cheeks blushed, and his whole complexion overall became blotchy and mottled.

He gave the receptionist an unconvincing smile:

'I'm alright...it's nothing really'

He took another step and continued his descent. She smiled back:

'Good evening then'

'Good evening'

He waved briefly, smiled again - and passed her reception desk. He held his briefcase in one hand and pushed the main entrance door open, that led directly onto the pavement outside, with the other.

She watched him leave before continuing to wrap up her own work for the day.

He only had a sock on one of his feet - that's not like Geoff!

She shook her head - bemused at eccentricity…

Chapter Twenty-Seven

It was a nostalgic return to *Bathcombe Bay* for Davieson - the delightful coastal resort where he had made a national name for himself.

A reporter or journalist had famously found Agatha Christie in the 1920's and brought an end to one of the largest police manhunts of the day. Well, he was a reporter - and he had helped the police too!

Yes, it was good to be back, and he had an idea to work through whilst he was there this time.

He had remembered every twist and turn, as the narrow lanes snaked out of the countryside, over the cliff-top headland - and gently down to the enchanting resort and beach promenade.

Davieson parked up on the seafront and first went to order fish and chips - open in a tray, to stave off his hunger. He liberally doused them in vinegar, sprinkled plenty of salt over the top of them (*probably too much he knew*), stabbed a chip with the small wooden fork - and popped it (steaming profusely) into his open mouth.

He blew out through his still open mouth, to cool it quickly and grinned.

No, there's nothing quite like fresh fish and chips at the seaside.

He sat down on the promenade wall, with his back to the sea. There were brightly-coloured benches - with unobstructed sea views aplenty, but he specifically wanted to watch the entrance to *The Grand Hotel*, whilst he ate.

Suitably fed, the Welshman discarded the tray and fork in a litter bin, checked his watch - and sat patiently for a further two minutes.

Presently the revolving door sprang into motion, and the receptionist appeared at the end of her shift.

Davieson jumped to his feet and slowly crossed the road towards her:

'Excuse me, madam!'

She wasn't expecting this stranger to have spoken to her, and flinched slightly. She eyed him suspiciously:

'Yes??'

'You kindly put this description together, to help the police locate a woman they are keen to speak with'

The stranger produced *The Morning Chronicle* from under his arm, thrust the front page towards her face - and pointed to the photo-fit.

She shot it a quick glance, and then looked back up at the stranger expectantly:

'Have they found her??'

He shook his head:

'Not that I'm aware of sorry'

'I don't understand then...who are you??'

'Merv Davieson - *The Morning Chronicle*. This is my story here'

He again pointed to the newspaper.

'Ok - so what do you want with me?'

The Welshman pointed down the promenade towards a beach cafe:

'Can I buy you a coffee and we can chat?'

She checked her watch and nodded:

'Sure'

The two of them made their way to a traditional beachfront cafe. Davieson ordered them two dubious coffees and they sat down, overlooking the beach.

He produced a notepad and biro from his blazer jacket.

'The description of the girl is excellent - and I'm sure it will soon pay dividends now everyone has woken up to read this today...but tell me about Mr. errr - *Smith*. What was he wearing please?'

The receptionist swallowed her mouthful of coffee and put it down on the table, confused:

'What was *he* wearing?? What good is that?...the police have found his body - there's nobody to try and locate and speak with there!'

'I appreciate that madam. Call it journalistic curiosity, if you like - and, to quote a common claim oft used by the tabloids...giving readers that exclusive *The Full Story*'

'Well a pale green summer jacket'

Davieson nodded and smiled. He scribbled on his notepad.

'Specifically what type of jacket would you say?'

'Well I'm no fashion expert, but I'd say a pale green *Summer Tweed* jacket. Not too heavy..you know??'

'I know the type yes. What else??'

'A check shirt'

'With a tie??'

Davieson grabbed the knot on his own slackened-off green tie to emphasise the question of detail.

'No - open at the neck'

'I see. And what about trousers?'

'*Trousers??* Let me think...tan *chinos*'

Davieson tapped the nib of his pen absently against the notepad. He had stopped recording proper notes a couple of questions previously, and was simply going through the motions, hearing his ideas and thoughts confirmed by this most useful and observant girl sharing a coffee with him.

He smiled at her warmly.

He didn't need any further notes - he had seen Peter Chapman wearing these described articles of clothing with his own eyes...lying dead in them when they had found him on the floor of his kitchen...

Chapter Twenty-Eight

She passed a half-full cycle rack - took a deep breath...and entered the imposing building.

What could this mean for her? What might they do with her? What could they do??

She decided to bite the bullet, and made straight for the front desk where there was a man stationed who was staring down at paperwork. A *duty sergeant* she assumed - if the many televised police dramas she had watched over the years, bore any resemblance to a truthful depiction of life inside a police station.

He hadn't noticed her arrival at the desk so she gave an *ahem* cough, to attract his attention. He promptly looked up in a start, and smiled widely at her...*a little too creepily for her own liking*!

'Can I help you, madam?'

'I need to speak to a....*Chief Inspector Kent*, I believe??'

'You do, do you, madam?'

'I believe so, yes'

'And what would this be regarding, please? - he's a very busy man madam'

Jodi Fletcher produced the copy of *The Morning Chronicle* she had brought with her, and placed it down firmly on the front desk in front of him.

The duty sergeant stared at it.

'This lady you're all searching for here'

She pointed:

'She's me..'

***

It was a couple of hours later when Kent phoned *The Morning Chronicle* offices and got hold of Davieson:

'Hello'

'Hello, Davieson. I wanted to say thank you'

'*Thank you,* Chief Inspector??'

'Yes. That photo-fit you kindly ran for us...well we've located the young lady within a day of publication, so it's been a great result thanks'

'Excellent - I'm glad to have been of help'

'Yes, she errr...came to us voluntarily - but on the back of attracting an inordinate amount of undue attention to herself, as a result of her mugshot being plastered all over your front cover'

'Well, your boys must have composed and compiled a good likeness then Chief Inspector. It was their craftsmanship...I just included it with my article'

'Nevertheless - good work Davieson. The case continues to progress in earnest again, and she's helped us manage to narrow down the final movements of Peter Chapman somewhat'

'The *story* Chief Inspector...the *story*!'

'*Story*??'

'You said *case*'

Kent sounded slightly flustered:

'...Well, story for you perhaps - case for the law!'

'Relax Chief Inspector - I'm teasing you'

'Oh...right'

'Anyway...who is she?'

'One Jodi Fletcher...single!'

'Her *relationship* to Peter Chapman then??'

'Fleeting!'

'*Fleeting*??'

'Yes. She says she'd only recently met him (we think she's telling the truth) and they met at a bar in *Haverton* one Saturday night. Peter Chapman approached her and she thought there was, quote - *something about him!*'

'There was something about him alright' agreed Davieson.

'Yes. Well, he's convinced her that he's some sort of local sports celebrity. She's fallen *hook, line and sinker* for that line...and his physical looks no doubt - and the next thing she knows is, she's agreed to accompany him on a dirty weekend at the seaside...despite knowing that he was a fair number of years older than her and that she should have known better'

'You said she's helped you narrow down Peter Chapman's final movements...so what do we now know?'

'Well according to Miss Fletcher, these two lovebirds made the most of their long weekend in *Bathcombe Bay*. They stayed there enjoying the sunshine until late afternoon, said their goodbyes on the seafront - and then headed their separate ways home after a *lovely* weekend together, avoiding all the earlier tourist traffic.

She claims she never saw him again!'

'No?'

'No. She says that she thought he would have been back in touch with her, either the very next day - or certainly sometime later in the week...but no call came.

She says she therefore first felt a little *used* - felt a little cheap in herself, then cheered herself up and told herself that he must just have been really busy with work.

Anyway. By the *Friday* ,July 12th, she says that she could stand it no longer, so she decided to take the initiative - and surprise him by turning up at his place unannounced'

'*And??*'

'And nothing! She says that he never answered his door'

'And what do you make of that Chief Inspector?'

'Well - that he didn't answer his door because he was lying dead in his kitchen, in a pool of blood by then!'

'I agree, Chief Inspector...I agree. What did she say she did then?'

'Says she drove home and thought she'd try to get back in touch with him another day'

'Ok, so you have an account from her perspective - but what do you think Peter Chapman did after he said goodbye at the seafront?'

'Well, we think he then drove home, parked his car in the garage sometime early that Sunday evening...'

'...And grabbed a cheese sandwich supper??' suggested Davieson mischievously.

The Welshman muffled the mouthpiece on the telephone so that Kent could not hear his laughter. His eyes sparkled in merriment.

The tall policeman blushed, and the line at the *Police Headquarters* end fell silent for a moment. Davieson could well imagine Kent's humble embarrassment, and was just about to rescue him when Kent spoke again:

'Errr no - we had the lab results back, and it's now clear that Peter Chapman had not consumed a cheese sandwich in the run-up to his death. Errr...thank you for the tip!'

'My pleasure Chief Inspector - so maybe the murderer ate it then??'

'I think you're dead right there Davieson...unfortunately it won't help us much though I'm afraid!'

'Oh??'

'No - the remnants of any cheese sandwich would be well out of a murderer's digestive system by now you see, so we'd be unable (at this late stage) to collate any meaningful gastral evidence to tie them into having been in Peter Chapman's kitchen on that basis alone, unfortunately. No, we'd need different evidence to be able to do that'

'Such as the boot print maybe??'

'Maybe Davieson - just maybe'

'Did you establish what size boot??'

'We did Davieson. We managed to identify the brand from the pattern of the tread, and from there managed to establish with the manufacturer that it was a print from a size eleven boot'

'Well that's something to go on Chief Inspector'

'It is indeed. Anyway, got to dash I'm afraid, Davieson - Sergeant Jones is after me...'

Chapter Twenty-Nine

'What is it, Jones?'

Sergeant Jones had half a foot in Kent's office. He stepped out from behind the door, and entered the room proper:

'There a lady downstairs, asking for you Chief Inspector'

'Who is she?'

'She says that it's in relation to the photo-fit, on the front of this paper here'

Jones waved a copy of the previous day's *Morning Chronicle* at his superior officer.

'Another one! Is she a twin?'

'A *twin* sir??'

'Nevermind Jones. Well if ladies are going to drop in, asking for us every few hours or so, to help us advance the case - then this just might be the most successful manhunt we've launched to date' concluded Kent: 'We must use Davieson more often!'

'*Ladyhunt* sir' corrected the sergeant'

Kent glared daggers at him:

'Yes - thank you, Jones. That will be all...I'll be down in a jiffy'

Suitably reprimanded, Jones decided that he would not risk *talking out of turn* again and quietly headed downstairs, leaving the Chief Inspector to join him in his own time.

Kent was not long, and soon he and Jones were sat down opposite Rebecca Chapman.

The woman looked nothing like Jodi Fletcher...she was much older too.

'Right then madam. I am Chief Inspector Kent - and this is Sergeant Jones, who will assist me. Now, let's start with your name please?'

'Rebecca...Rebecca Chapman'

Did she detect the two policeman exchange a brief glance at each other??

'Ok. And I understand that you want to tell us something about this lady here - is that right?'

Kent placed the copy of *The Chronicle* in front of her, that the lady had herself brought into *Police Headquarters* with her.

She nodded:

'That's right, yes'

'And what is it you wish to tell us please madam?'

'That I've seen her recently'

'Are you sure?'

'I'm positive...the likeness is remarkable'

'And when was this please madam?'

'It was the 12th July...it was a Friday'

Kent flicked open his diary:

'It was indeed madam. And what time of day was this please?'

'It wasn't the day as such - it was the evening'

'I see. And where did you see this lady that evening then please?'

'At the home of Peter Chapman'

The two policemen definitely looked at each other this time. The taller man taking the lead whistled audibly.

'Same surname...any relation??'

He knew the answer - he wanted her to confirm it herself.

Her head dipped. She had a melancholic look about her:

'Yes. He was my estranged husband'

'Was he now? Well, I'm sorry for your loss madam - this must be difficult for you?'

She snorted involuntarily:

'Well it's difficult plucking up the courage to come here to a police station...of my own volition I'll add - but a loss?? No - I don't consider Peter's passing a loss'

'I see. But equally, you wouldn't have wished what actually happened to him, on him?...*would you??*'

'I guess not' she confessed.

'*You guess not??*'

'No, of course not - just ignore me please, I'm rambling'

'Just rambling...I see madam'
He didn't.

'And what were you doing at the home of your estranged husband then madam?'

She looked confused:

'Me?? - well, I wasn't there!'

'I thought you just told us you saw this lady in the newspaper there? Am I missing something??'

'No it's perfectly simple. She was there...and I wasn't'

Kent looked at Sergeant Jones and raised his own eyebrows. He looked back at Rebecca Chapman:

'So how did you see her there then madam?'

'Well I was parked up near the house'

'Parked up where exactly?'

'There's a lay-by near the end of his drive - next to the woods there'

'Ah, we've seen the one - haven't we Jones?'

The sergeant nodded.

'Going for a walk were you?'

'Errr no'

'So why were you parked there, madam?'

She looked embarrassed. She admitted as much herself:

'It's kind of embarrassing'

'Well don't worry madam - the walls are thick in this interview room here, and we promise not to poke fun at you...don't we Jones?'

His tone was reassuring and Jones again dutifully nodded.

'Well I was trying to discreetly keep an eye on him'

'And do you regularly keep your, errr...*eye* on other people madam??'

'Only Peter...well I did I mean!'

'Ok, so we've established that you were spying on Peter Chapman...'

'Keeping my eye on him' cut in Rebecca Chapman.

'...*Spying* on him' emphasised Kent determinedly: 'So why were you spying on him please?'

'I thought you wanted to know about this lady??' she said defensively, and pointed to the newspaper.

'We do madam, we do indeed - but I'm trying to understand the circumstances in which you saw her, and ensure that you're a credible witness if we manage to locate her'

He prayed the two ladies hadn't passed each other on their respective ways to and from Police Headquarters.

'Well Peter and I had only just separated - and whilst he hadn't admitted there was someone else as such, there were rumours abound at our cricket club, that he was now seeing the other lady who makes the teas with me on matchdays'

'The cricket club at *Upper Woodleigh*'

'Yes'

'And who is this other lady please?'

'Deborah Knowles'

'Make a note of that please Jones'

The sergeant scribbled away.

'What, and you wanted to confirm if these rumours were true right??'

'Yes'

'And if they were??'

'Well, I'd have had it out with Peter of course!'

'*You'd have had it out with Peter*...how would that have gone madam?'

'Well, I'd have given him an earful!'

'Anything else?

She suddenly realised that she was incriminating herself somewhat:

'No comment'

'Ok - so you were discreetly spying on him - what did you see?'

'Well, not her!'

'Not this lady??'

Kent pointed to the *Morning Chronicle* again.

'No - not Deborah Knowles'

'But you saw this younger lady instead...is that right?'

'She's not that much younger than me!'

'Errr no, madam. But you saw her?'

'Yes'

'What was she doing?'

'Well she parked up, sat for a minute or two in her car on his drive - then stepped out with a bottle of wine in her hand, and headed for Peter's front door'

'What then?'

'Well he didn't let her in, so she came back to her car, got in - and drove off'

'What did you do?'

'I waited for her to drive off'

'And what then?'

'Well I drove back to my parents'

'Will they corroborate that?'

'They would - but go easy on them, they're elderly'

'Well we will do if we need to do that...it may be unnecessary madam'

'Thank you'

'Have you seen this lady since?'

'No'

'Anything else you can tell us at all please?'

'I don't think so'

'Are you a...religious person madam?' probed Kent, as slowly and gently as he could get the words out.

She shrugged:

'I guess so – why?'

'Nevermind. Well thank you for providing this information madam - leave us an address we can contact you at and we'll be in touch if we need you further'

She left her parent's details and proceeded to leave the room. She paused at the door, put her hand to her head - and wheeled round:

'Oh, I just remembered something else - it nearly slipped my mind sorry'

'Yes??'

'Yes, some maniac nearly clipped wing mirrors with me as I drove away'

'Some *maniac*??'

'Yes. Speeding - driving in the middle of the road...clearly deranged! I got properly annoyed I did and swore loudly to myself'

Rebecca Chapman was evidently one of those kinds of women, who get themselves het up, angry and annoyed...retelling a situation when they had been het up, angry and annoyed!

'Do you know who this *deranged* maniac might be?'

'Well, I couldn't be positive...'

'But??'

'Well, it looked like it might have been Rebecca Knowles' husband, Andrew'

'What does he drive?'

'Well, I don't know what he drives exactly. But if it was him...'

'Yes madam'

'...Then I think I got at least half the registration number. I was furious that he could have killed me you see, and so I looked back in my rearview mirror and I made a mental note of at least half of the registration number. I was looking at a reflection of course, so my head wasn't working fast enough for me to note any more as he sped off I'm afraid. I scribbled what I could make out down on a sheet of paper back at my parents'

Rebecca Chapman fumbled in her handbag and gave them the sheet of paper...

Chapter Thirty

Geoffrey Wright turned his maroon four-wheel drive vehicle clumsily into his drive. He revved the engine violently when he had intended to gently brake.

The drive home - shod in only one shoe had not been a pleasant affair, and the sole of his left foot throbbed where it had interacted with the car's pedals.

The agony had dulled his other senses and held his full attention. He hadn't even noticed the car parked outside his property as he had turned in.

'Hello again Mr. Wright'

His heart sank when he saw the Chief Inspector - and the other fellow with him too.

'Have you brought my shoe back?'

'Your *shoe??*...No, it's your book collection we've come to see sir!'

'My *book collection*??'

'That's right sir - can we come in?'

'Do I have a choice??'

The Chief Inspector did not respond.

He unlocked the front door and the three of them entered the house.

'So where do you keep your books, sir?'

'They're in my study...it's this way'

They followed Geoffrey Wright into a small room lined wall to wall with shelves of books. The volumes of both antique buckram-bound books - and modern cheaper paperbacks was vast.

Kent put his hands on his hips and craned his neck to scan the contents of Geoffrey Wright's personal library - something he must have collated over many many years. He looked overwhelmed at the sheer number of titles present before his eyes.

Simpkins came to his rescue and tapped his shoulder:

'There's one just there look sir'

Kent looked at where his sergeant had spotted and indicated a *King James* version of *The Bible*.

He raised his eyes satisfied:

'Bag it please Simpkins'.

He'd leaf through Geoffrey Wright's Bible in some detail back at Police Headquarters, to see if he could ascertain the former cricket umpire's reading habits - and in doing so, make any correlation with the passages of scripture Davieson had kindly pulled together for him.

Geoffrey Wright felt that they were gradually wearing him down. He was issued a further receipt...

***

Back at *Police Headquarters*, Kent found Sergeant Jones anxiously waiting to speak to him.

'How has it been going Jones?'

'Well I've obtained plenty of samples sir'

'That doesn't sound *overly* reassuring Jones - did you get them all?'

'Not all sir'

'*Will you* get them all Jones?'

Sergeant Jones nodded enthusiastically:

'I will sir'

'Good man!'

'Anything of key interest on your travels?'

'I think so sir'

'Go on??'

He'd aroused the Chief Inspector's interest.

'Well the size elevens are reaping little reward sir - but just a shoe size away (size ten)...and we have three of your person's of interest!'

'Oh yeah?'

'Yes, sir...Bob Butler, John Middleton and Craig Ellsmere all take a size ten shoe'

'...But none of them an eleven?'

'No sir'

He thought that Kent did not look particularly pleased!

***

It was the Wednesday evening. Craig Ellsmere walked into the lounge bar at *Upper Woodleigh Cricket Club* pavilion and made straight for Bob Butler at the bar, to order himself a drink. *It was sounding like he might need one if the summons was anything to go by!*

The barman raised his eyebrows.

Craig turned around and saw that a table had been commandeered for committee use. He saw John Middleton theatrically inspecting his wristwatch, at the head of it. It was 5:58 p.m.

'Good evening Craig. We're just waiting for Alan now - and then we'll begin'

'I've just passed him - he'll be here in a minute'

The outside door could be heard opening, as soon as Craig took one of the three remaining free chairs for himself, and in walked Alan:

'Mind if I get myself a quick?...'

He motioned to a smiling Bob at the bar.

'Go on' said John, shaking his head - and with a hint of resignation: '...just be quick about it please'

'Thank you, John - will do'

Bob Butler poured the Secretary a quick pint. He was rushing, and the head-to-ale ratio was not what Alan would have ideally wanted - but he didn't push his luck, and took a seat at the table...frothy pint in hand.

Bob joined him, and they were a full compliment by 6:02.

Several pairs of eyes looked at John Middleton expectantly.

He duly obliged them...he was prepared:

'Gentleman. The way I see things...from my position as Chairman of this fine cricket club of ours, is that Peter Chapman had been systematically undoing our goodwill, tarnishing our reputation and standing, and making the lives of both players on the field - and officials (such as our good selves here tonight) an absolute misery!

No wonder *County* didn't sign him - despite his obvious talents with the ball.

The man was a nasty bully, arrogant, a womaniser...with no respect for the feelings, emotions - or reputations, of the fairer sex - and, from what I hear, he was unscrupulous and showed little mercy in business too. I believe he has sadly *screwed many an honest businessman over!*

And lo - despite him now having been wiped off the face of this good earth - his name...and that of *Upper Woodleigh Cricket Club,* more to the point, is sadly plastered all over the front pages of the daily tabloids!

Gentlemen, I have therefore summoned you here tonight to discuss what we are going to do about *this* matter - and how do we eradicate this blot (I mean Peter Chapman!) from all of this?...'

John Middleton swept an arm around the room and pointed to the glass trophy cabinet, gilt-framed cricketing photographs - and range of pennants that proudly adorned the walls of the lounge bar around them.

The other committee members looked around - some of them nodded gently, a determined look on their faces. They were in full agreement with their Chairman, and his passionate opening statement.

'Well, I spend most of my time in here. It's not as if we haven't plenty of other memorabilia to show off...so I could tactfully *lose* all the team photographs he appears in, and arrange for his name to be struck off our bowling honours board' began Bob.

The others nodded enthusiastically.

'I like it...good start!' agreed John.

'And I could check that the youngster we played last game, is happy to step up on a more permanent basis to the 1st XI' offered Craig: '...he played an absolute blinder on his debut'

'So I hear, so I hear - yes, good one. Let's quickly demonstrate, to the *Haverton & District Cricket League,* that we certainly aren't missing Peter...and never will be!'

'And another thing I'll tell you all - Danny never dropped a single catch last game! We've improved in that department too' added Craig.

'He must have coated his hands in treacle' joked Bob.

They laughed.

'Our Captain makes another valid point gentleman' interjected John: 'Take away the pressure - take away Peter Chapman's bullying and intimidation, and Danny is more relaxed and confident too!'

'I'll be honest, it allowed me a clearer head too - not having my tactics and fielding positions constantly criticised...I haven't enjoyed a game as much in years!' admitted Craig.

'What about the friction he caused amongst our good ladies making the teas?' asked Ted.

'Yes - a tricky situation there...especially as we have a home fixture this weekend. Are there any of our better halves who could lend a hand there and help them out?? I'm thinking that planting a neutral party in there with them, might diffuse any animosity - and lead to a more harmonious and happy teas team...our teas are the envy of the league after all!'

'I could ask my wife' suggested Craig.

'Would you please Craig? It'd be great if she could help...I'd ask my own wife - but she's arranged to visit her mother this weekend'

'Sure, no problem'

'Thank you, Craig. On the subject of Saturday's fixture...'

The Chairman left the line hanging in the air, as the various faces of *Upper Woodleigh Cricket Club Committee* stared back at him expectantly.

'...I'm looking for that to be the end of Peter Chapman!'

'But he's already dead' snorted Bob.

He looked round with mischievous eyes, feeling rather pleased with himself at the witticism - and checking that the others were all laughing along with him.

'I mean that I'm going to rule a line firmly under him (his name) at the game this weekend. I'll pull together some sort of appropriate speech - deliver it on our behalf, say all the right things...and then I don't expect to hear any of us mentioning his name much ever again! Understood??'

'Y-yeah' agreed Ted enthusiastically, and rushing his response.

The others nodded agreement.

'Good. Anyway, my next thought - was that on the back of all these events, that well-worn phrase *If only I could turn back the clock* sprang to mind. I guess you're all as keen as me, to try and return to the happy place we were in before Peter Chapman ever came on the scene?'

They again nodded.

'We can't physically turn back time of course - but it'd be great if we could make things feel as they were before *Chapman*'

'Have you anything in mind in particular John?' enquired Bob.

'Well, I wondered if we might be able to get Roger Lenton back down the club?'

Alan Chambers shook his head doubtfully:

'I very much doubt it, John. Roger's become a complete recluse'

There was disappointment - tinged with wistful regret, painted all across John Middleton's face. The table fell silent as he locked eyes with Alan, and pressured the latter into speaking further:

'...I could ask him if you like. But no promises - I'm not hopeful'

'Well let's try Alan. Tell Roger our aims. Tell him we'd all love to see him back here - and see what he says'

'Will do John'

They paused for a second round of drinks and stretched their legs whilst Bob processed the orders.

Resuming again - and all back in their chairs, they were largely finished, halfway down their second pints.

'Is there any other business?'

They flicked eyes at each other, but no one spoke and all shook their heads silently.

'Good. Well that's us finished then'

They prepared to rise from their chairs.

'...Oh, just one final thing gentlemen'

They paused mid-rise.

'...Please be careful when you speak to the press. They're obviously on our patch and fishing for comments. That Welsh fellow isn't too bad - but some of the tabloid coverage is appalling, sensationalist and delving into grubby details that are not in keeping with the fine name we at least *had* here at *Upper Woodleigh Cricket Club*! So remember...*Upper Woodleigh* first - your own private thoughts and prejudices second. Understood??'

There were several coloured faces looking back at John Middleton. They looked uncomfortable but nodded their assent...

Chapter Thirty-One

The car was parked in the driveway.

Kent came to a halt at the bottom of it and placed his hands on his hips.

Sergeant Jones thought that he should halt too - and follow the Chief Inspector's lead as and when that would be required. His superior spoke:

'Well half the number plate matches for sure Jones...looks like Rebecca Chapman is an attentive sort alright - and a reliable witness, should she be called upon to give evidence in court. Let's see what Mr. Knowles has to say for himself shall we?'

Jones nodded in agreement, and the two continued up the driveway to the *Knowles'* front door.

Andrew Knowles himself answered the door. All traces of the black eye Peter Chapman had inflicted upon him, had long since faded and disappeared.

'Andrew Knowles??'

'That's right'

Kent flashed his credentials:

'Chief Inspector Kent - and Sergeant Jones...can we come in please sir?'

'Errr, sure...this way'

The two policemen followed him into the house. He looked nervous.

'What's this about?'

Kent and Jones looked at each other and briefly raised synchronised eyebrows:

'Well, what do you think this is about sir?'

'Sorry...stupid of me. I guess this is about Peter, right??'

'That's right sir. Peter Chapman! One of your cricketing chums I believe?'

'Well, we played together in the same village side if that's what you're implying?'

'Not a chum then?'

'I suppose I wouldn't say that we were on the best of terms, no'

'And yet you were seen in the vicinity of Peter Chapman's barn conversion on the evening of Friday the 12th of July sir...can you explain what you were doing there?'

'Say's who??'

'We're asking the questions sir'

'Sorry...I apologise'

'Thank you, sir. So what were you doing there?'

Andrew Knowles put his left hand up to his head and ran his fingers absently through flowing locks. Kent thought he looked stressed...*he was definitely worried.* He puffed his cheeks out and exhaled audibly:

'Better to come clean I guess!'

'Always better to come clean in a murder enquiry sir'

Sergeant Jones prepared to start and make notes in earnest.

'Well I was actually driving over there to have words with him'

'...*Words??*'

'Yes. I was going to give him a piece of my mind'

'I see. And why exactly were you going to give him a piece of your mind may I ask?'

He looked injured and embarrassed.

'Well things haven't been great between my wife and I for a little while now, and rumours had started to circulate that she was having an affair with Peter Chapman'

'...Sorry - your wife is?'

'Deborah...Deborah Knowles'

'Thank you sir - and sorry to interrupt you in full flow. Please continue'

'Yes, well I finally got some sort of proof that the rumours were true, and confronted him about it'

'On the 12th?'

'No this was earlier - after practice in the nets...and after a few too many beers I'm afraid. I needed plenty of *Dutch courage* to pluck up the confidence to confront him you see...he was quite a forceful character!'

'So we understand sir. So when exactly did you confront him?'

'Let me see. Well, nets are on Thursday evenings, so it would have been the 4th'

'What did you say to him?'

'I told him to stay away from Deborah'

'And what did Peter Chapman have to say to that?'

'Well he let his fists do the talking, and it quickly turned nasty!'

'Oh yes??'

'Yes - we had a fight I'm ashamed to say'

'Where was this please sir?'

'In the lounge bar at the cricket pavilion'

'Were there witnesses?'

Andrew Knowles scoffed:

'Witnesses??...there was a bar full in there. The others had to pull us apart, as there was glass and beer flying all over the place...I apologised to our barman, Bob, afterwards'

'So where does the 12th come into things, sir? I thought you had said your piece at the club??'

'Ah, well I woke up the next morning with a black eye and sore head, and the more I reflected on things - the more it felt like we had been pulled apart prematurely'

'...So you wanted a rematch?'

Kent smiled at Sergeant Jones, and at his own joke.

'If you like, yes'

'An *eye for an eye* eh?'

'Sorry??'

'Nevermind. And so you drove over to his place on the 12th?'

'Well I did eventually...but that wasn't my original plan'

'No??'

'No - I thought I'd speak to him at our home game on the Saturday.

'The 6th?'

'Yes'

'*And?*'

'Well he wasn't playing'

'And you didn't know that?'

'No. Our captain, Craig, selects the side you see'

'Craig??'

'Ellsmere'

'I see. And so you went round to his on the 12th?'

'Well only because he wasn't at *nets* the following Thursday either!'

Kent shook his head and snorted'

'*If at first, you don't succeed* eh?'

'Something like that'

'So you go round to Peter Chapman's place (your fourth attempt I might add) in some sort of aggressive...mood, say - and of a somewhat confrontational disposition, and I imagine that you were getting more irate by each missed opportunity to *have it out* with him, that passed...so what happened with attempt number four?'

'Well he didn't answer the door, did he'

'Was his car there?'

'*His car*?? Let me think...I don't think so, no'

'So what did you do?'

'Well I got back into my car, and drove away'

'You sure about that?'

'Yes I'm sure'

'Can anyone vouch for that?'

'I was on my own that time, so no...it wasn't like the fight in the pavilion'

'You didn't break into his house and decide to wait for him there then?'

'No - I haven't broken into anywhere!'

'Ok, sir. One last thing (for now). You mentioned that you finally got proof that Peter Chapman had been having an affair with your wife. What proof??'

'Well I watched his house to see if I could catch Deborah visiting him there'

'And you saw her there?'

'I did, yes'

'How many times did you watch the house, before you got this evidence?'

'I dunno...half a dozen times I guess'

'Half a dozen??'

'There or thereabouts'

'I see. So you certainly had your *eye* on him then wouldn't you say!'

'I guess so, yes'

'And where were you watching the house from?'

'There's a lay-by near the bottom of his driveway, next to *Rowley Woods*. You can discreetly watch his house from there and remain largely inconspicuous'

'Yes we're getting to know the lay-by quite well, aren't we Jones?...'

Chapter Thirty-Two

Davieson parked up, grabbed his sun hat off the empty passenger seat, and opened the boot of his car. He retrieved the lunch box, flask - and blue and white-striped deckchair he had loaded into the car earlier, and made for the cricket boundary where other spectators had already made camp.

Upper Woodleigh Cricket Club had their first home fixture since the discovery of Peter Chapman's mutilated body had been shared with the community and wider world!

Folestree Magna were the day's visitors.

Davieson had no trouble at all in convincing his Editor that he should quite rightly *plant himself in the heart of the matter at hand* and spend a good day *in the field*, whilst he pursued a story that had by now gathered national interest. For Davieson that meant a legitimate opportunity to mix business with pleasure, and he was as much looking forward to relaxing and watching a good game of cricket - as he was sniffing out any comment, gossip or developing storyline.

He spotted Chief Inspector Kent and Sergeant Jones...both in plain clothes, already seated just shy of the boundary and decided to pitch up next to them.

'Morning Chief Inspector!...Sergeant Jones'

He nodded to both, grabbed his Panama cricket hat - and raised it several inches above his head.

Kent looked anxiously around himself in brief panic, but there was no one in earshot:

'Errr - we're here incognito Davieson!'

'Oh. Of course...I do apologise'

'No harm done Davieson - but M*um's the word* from now on eh?'

'Absolutely...errr - Kent'

'That'll do'

'Anyway, I'm off to the pavilion bar to get myself a beer - would you like a drink?'

'We're sorted thanks, Davieson - but thank you'

Kent nodded down at their feet. The Welshman noted a pint of beer stood at the foot of Kent...a small orange juice at that of Sergeant Jones.

He assembled his deckchair and set it up next to Kent. He then put his lunch box and flask on the grass next to it, and with that - headed off to the bar. It was getting busier by the minute - an above-average crowd keen to watch the amateur cricket side that the whole nation was now talking about!

There were a few in, so he queued patiently behind others already waiting, whilst Bob Butler did his best to serve all as quickly and as politely as he could.

As he stepped up to the bar, Davieson quickly perused the beer pumps on offer that day. He looked back up to the barman:

'Ah...hello again. I'm delighted you've still got that real ale on...it was a lovely pint, so I'll have one of those please'

'Righto, sir. It's plastic glasses today though on match day...committee rules I'm afraid'

The Welshman rolled his eyes and smiled, as Bob Butler prized another disposable and cheap plastic pint glass from a stacked tower that must have contained a dozen or more:

'Committees eh?...who is on the committee, setting the rules here then??'

'Well, I am sir...'

'Oh'

Davieson looked embarrassed.

'....and our Chairman, Secretary, Groundsman, Captain etc. Some of us are more stringent and officious than others of course - and we almost all of us have our own opinion as to what is the correct and right way to go about things. Committee meetings are an ordeal I can tell you...one could quite, quite easily lose the will to live before *Any Other Business*!'

Davieson chuckled:

'I can quite imagine'

'Anyway, did that, errr - Chief Inspector catch up with you?'

Davieson briefly (and involuntarily) glanced over his shoulder towards the cricket field before he checked himself:

'Errr, he did yes thank you'

'Good job - kept pestering me for something I never had, he did'

Davieson blushed:

'Yes. sorry - a misunderstanding, and my mistake'

'Nevermind - there you go sir'

The barman set the pint down before him on a beer towel. The plastic glass buckled slightly, under the pressure of Bob Butler's fingers, and the creamy head came flooding over the rim and trickling down the sides of the glass. *It already did not look nearly half as an appealing pint, as that he had enjoyed on his first visit there.*

The Welshman took a leisurely sip of his pint but did not move away from the bar. No one had entered the bar, so no one was as yet waiting to be served.

'Peter Chapman eh?...he must be a tremendous loss to you all here at *Upper Woodleigh?*'

Bob Butler snorted:

'Well takings will be down for starters (that's for sure!) The *club* will certainly miss that...but no, I won't miss him sir!'

'Big drinker was he??'

The barman shook his head:

'It wasn't so much that - more any opportunity to flash his cash and flaunt his obvious wealth in people's faces really. He'd have a good spell of overs in the field...then he'd buy champagne for *us all* to celebrate later.

We had to join in of course, for good order!

And if there was an audience or good crowd in, he'd be quick to buy the most expensive wines (he'd drink us dry of all the good stuff) and the most expensive spirits on offer - attracting the most amount of attention to himself he could engineer. You know?...the aged malts, the rare vintage brandy - the artisan gins. Got right up most people's noses, I can tell you!'

'You said *for starters*??'

'Well yes, then there's the aggro as well you see. If it was a public house...rather than a private bar, then he'd be barred by now! I'd have barred him myself - but my fellow committee members wouldn't have it...scared and all too aware that he bankrolls the club I guess'

'*Aggro*??'

'His tongue for one - a regular wind-up merchant and a bully. Constantly dishing out little digs at anyone he fancied...but he couldn't take the equivalent back himself. That's the reason we've had so many fights and broken glass in here.

We were always pulling him and some other (usually entirely innocent) victim of his apart...it was poor old Andrew Knowles turn just the other day!'

Davieson remembered the name from the scorecard he had briefly had in his possession, just as two elderly gentlemen entered the room and made for the bar. He made his excuses and departed:

'Well, must dash - my friends will be wondering where I have gotten to'

Back with Kent and Jones, Davieson set his plastic pint glass down carefully on the grass, slumped in his deckchair with a satisfying sigh, prised open his lunchbox - and promptly waved it under the nose of Chief Inspector Kent:

'Cheese and Beetroot sandwich anyone??'

Kent looked down at *very* homemade sandwiches, made on white bread stained purple with blotches of seeping beetroot juice that had permeated from somewhere within!'

He screwed his face up, despite his best endeavours to mask his emotions:

'Errr no thank you Davieson'

'You Jones??'

'I'm good thanks' declined Kent's sergeant.

'Suit yourselves gentlemen - but they're terrific...I can assure you of that!'

'I'm sure they are Davieson' added Kent dryly: 'Anyway...you were a long time in there!'

Kent eyed him keenly - trying to read the journalist's face.

'Yeah - hell of a queue at the bar...everyone trying to get a pint in before play commences I guess'

Kent looked at him a moment more, but Davieson offered nothing extra:

'I guess so, yes'

'Anyway, Kent. I'm a big cricket fan...as you well know, and there's little I enjoy more than a relaxing day watching local cricket - indeed the grass roots of the great game...but what are you doing here? and what do you hope to achieve?'

'My superiors have made it quite clear, that there are to be no more bodies, no more mutilations - and no more, nasty cricketing accidents!!!'

'I see'

'Yes - and the best way I think I might be able to stop that happening is by being a dedicated *man on the ground* so to speak - and with a fair wind, maybe even catching our deviant at it (as it were) and stepping in to prevent further loss of life'

'A man *in the ground* today, wouldn't you say?'

'Hilarious Davieson' chuntered Kent miserably.

In due time, the two teams filed out of the pavilion to a round of polite applause. *Upper Woodleigh* (Craig Ellsmere) had won the toss and decided to put *Folestree Magna* in to bat.

Davieson clocked that three of the home side were carrying helmets...*current wicketkeeper and slips he guessed.* Both *Folestree Magna* opening batsmen wore helmets too. The accident consequences -

coupled with the inevitable *Health & Safety* repercussions, had reverberated throughout the *Haverton & District Cricket League*, and a new *best practice* had been widely adopted.

For the second game running, there was one noticeable absentee in the home team's line-up - *Upper Woodleigh's* star bowler, but regular spectators were pleased, at least, to see the inclusion once again of the youth team bowler who had made such a bright and promising debut in the previous game, and helped to fill a considerable void in their attacking prowess.

Many others filed out of the pavilion, behind the players, in a continual stream. A common sight as many would not want to miss the action - especially on a balmy day such as today.

There was an older chap, who Davieson *thought must be the groundsman*, two ladies wearing bib aprons - *the ladies who serve the players refreshments at lunch and tea??* They walked out together...but then promptly stood well apart - and finally Bob Butler, the barman.

Before play began, both teams assembled in front of the pavilion for a formal announcement followed by a minute's silence. Players, officials and spectators alike fell silent and maintained good order.

John Middleton, as Chairman, looked down at the speech, or words, he had been preparing, honing -

and deliberating over for half of the previous night. Davieson recognised him from various photographs and press cuttings he had perused on the walls of the lounge bar. Everyone else looked down at their shoes, their sandals...or the grass.

He also recognised Alan Chambers, Bob Butler and Craig Ellsmere amongst them - others he was sure must be faces attached to some of the names on the scorecard, which was now with Kent as an official case reference document.

As John Middleton began to address the assembly, Davieson studied them all thoughtfully, and assessed the body language on display, as the former continued on, and they listened to his words.

The Chairman, himself - and the Secretary stood tight at his side, appeared moved of a sort, respectful - and sympathetic, as the Chairman spoke of the *great loss Upper Woodleigh Cricket Club had suffered*.

The rest of them...well - general disinterestedness and disdain seemed to be the prevailing feeling amongst them. Many were nodding at all the right moments during John's speech, being seen to show the right response for the benefit of any casual observer, but...w*ere they faking it?*

Respects duly paid, *Upper Woodleigh* took up their fielding positions whilst the opposing batsman made their way to the crease. The umpire soon had play underway and the home team's youngster was soon quickly at them.

Davieson leisurely munched on his sandwiches and supped his pint (*he'd save his flask for tea later on*).

Several overs in to the match - and *Upper Woodleigh* already having their opponents three wickets down, the older chap - who Davieson had noticed earlier as everyone filed out of the pavilion, approached the three men and made straight for Kent.

'Excuse me, sir'

'Yes??'

'Errr...is it *Chief Inspector Kent??*'

Kent shot an irate glance at Davieson.

The latter put his hands defensively up into the air:

'Nothing to do with me'

Kent turned back to the gentleman who had spoken to him.

'Who's asking?' snapped the tall policeman.

'Hello, sir. I'm Ted Ellis...the groundsman here. I need to speak with you Chief Inspector...'

Chapter Thirty-Three

'This way please sir'

Kent and Sergeant Jones had decided to call a premature end to their planned day out at the cricket...given Ted Ellis eagerness to speak to them about a matter that *had been concerning him* - and instead chosen to bring him in with them to *Police Headquarters,* in order to make a formal statement away from prying eyes and unwelcome eavesdroppers.

They had left Davieson alone to enjoy the rest of the match...and his precious cheese and beetroot sandwiches!

In bringing him in, Chief Inspector Kent had to promise that he would have him returned to the cricket club by the close of play, after Ted had stressed at length the inordinate amount of important jobs that the groundsman has to see to, once the players and officials are enjoying a pint in the bar, and the spectators have long since returned home!

Ted Ellis was a martyr for the cause...and would tell anyone who would listen about it too!

They sat him in an interview room and took two seats opposite him:

'Well, what do you need to tell us then sir?'

Well I was preparing the ground for the previous home match...the first game that Peter Chapman missed, when I couldn't find some of the gear and kit, I regularly use to carry out the work'

'The *first game* sir??'

Ted Ellis shrugged his shoulders:

'Well, he couldn't very well play today either could he?'

Kent reddened:

'I'm sorry...no I guess not sir. So you couldn't find your gear???...' encouraged the tall policeman:

'Yes, that's right' continued Ted.

'And what items couldn't you find then, Mr. Ellis?'
Kent sounded disinterested.

'Well, I have a little running order, a preparing-for-work ritual if you like...'

Kent and Sergeant Jones smiled patiently

'Ok'

'...I sat myself down to put my *Wellington* boots on - as I always do first...I couldn't find them...'

'...Well, there's nothing too unusual in that Mr. Ellis - I'm always misplacing things myself, sir. Look - I'll be honest with you. There's not much for us to go on so far here sir - and we don't *really* get drafted in to locate misplaced *Wellington* boots!'

The Chief Inspector stood up to leave:

'I think you can take it from here Jones'

'I HADN'T misplaced them Chief Inspector!' snapped Ted Ellis.

He looked offended.

Kent sat back down:

'Ok...I'm sorry. Please do continue...'

'...Errr Chief Inspector!'

'What?'

Jones whispered quietly in his superior's ear. The latter shook himself:

'I'm sorry...awfully remiss of me - what shoe size are you sir?'

'My shoe size??'

'Yes, your shoe size please sir?'

'Well, an eleven...but I don't understand??'

Kent peered under the table at Ted Ellis' sizeable feet. *They were big indeed...not unlike his own:*

'Don't worry sir - may be helpful...if we can return the errr....*missing* goods to you, you see?'

'Oh I see, yes - righto'

'And when exactly was this then, please? - that you noticed the boots missing I mean?'

'It was the previous Thursday, Chief Inspector'

'And where were these boots normally stored?'

'In the storeroom at the pavilion...it's pretty much my own den there'

'Locked up??'

'Sometimes'

'Sometimes??'

'Well, when the pavilion is closed - or the storeroom not being used by me, I tend to lock it, yes, but it's a fairly good-natured and trustworthy sport...we've never had theft'

'What about on match day?'

'Theft??'

'Locking up!'

'Oh it would be open then'

'When would you lock up?'

'Not until close of play in the evening, and when everything was retrieved from the outfield - and safely packed back away in its place'

'Who else uses the storeroom?'

'Anyone who needs any gear - you know players when they're practising in the nets, and so on'

'I see. And if it was locked...who could open it?'

'Any member of the committee'

'The committee being??'

'Me, the Chairman, the Secretary, the barman, the Captain'...but they'd probably lend the keys to any official or player who needed access'

Kent screwed his face up as Jones took notes:

'So missing boots, in a room possibly left unlocked - and used by others?? Anyway - do continue. You say *gear* - not just boots, was other gear missing?...Tell us about that please sir'

'Yes. Well, then I came to look for my gardening gloves...I couldn't find them Chief Inspector. I then needed my shovel (we'd had an infestation of moles trying their united best to destroy the outfield you see)...I coul...'

'You couldn't find it!' cut in Kent: 'Wait a minute - a shovel you say?' *His ears pricked up and he shot a glance at Sergeant Jones:* 'Make a note of that please Jones!'

Had Ted Ellis' shovel been used to bury two hapless victims in Rowley Woods??

Kent continued:

'That's *very* interesting sir - were you missing more??'

'Yes - I would later find out that my screwdriver had disappeared too'

Jones continued to make notes and a detailed inventory.

'Anything else??'

'Yes - my turf aerating fork...'

Kent looked clueless:

'Come again??'

'My turf aerating fork'

The Chief Inspector shook his head mechanically from side to side. He looked at Sergeant Jones, who just shrugged his shoulders and offered no assistance:

'I'm sorry - I'm still none the wiser I'm afraid. What exactly is a, errr...*turf aerating fork*? - and what does this turf aerating fork look like sir?'

Ted Ellis smiled:

'I thought you might ask that so I bought the specialist catalogue in with me, from where we order the various equipment and supplies we require to maintain the ground to the standards it has become well-noted for'

The groundsman of *Upper Woodleigh Cricket Club* reached into a bag he had brought into *Police Headquarters* with him and produced a niche sales catalogue of limited appeal. He flicked through a page or two, swivelled the catalogue around on the desk between himself and the policemen, and pointed:

'It was one of those!'

Kent bent down to read the small print, comprising a product description in a *drainage* section of the catalogue:

3-Pronged Turf Aerating Fork with 7" solid tines. Regular use of the fork allows air and moisture to get to the grass roots, encourages grass root development...

Kent and Sergeant Jones looked at each other excitedly. *Surely they now knew exactly what had been used to kill the three victims, and why it had left such uniform wounds on their bodies.* Kent looked back at Ted Ellis:

'Fascinating' he lied (about the product itself at least!): 'May we keep this please?'

'Of course...anything to help'

'So give us a clue Mr. Ellis...who do *you* think might have taken these items?'

Ted Ellis snarled:

'Well, I'll admit that at first, I assumed it must have been that idiot, Peter Chapman! He was always beggaring around making mischief and winding everyone up. And it wouldn't have been the first time he's hidden mine or others' possessions. The number of times players have come back to the changing rooms to change back out of their whites, only to find their trousers had disappeared - or one sock was missing, you wouldn't believe! No, I didn't care for the man - and I wouldn't have put it past him'

Jones suppressed a smile.

'So maybe Peter Chapman??' clarified Kent.

'Yes...hey - you didn't find these items at his house did you??'

'No we didn't Mr. Ellis...'

Chapter Thirty-Four

As lunch loomed, Davieson thought that he would head inside for a refill a little early, and dodge the crowds before the bar queue became too busy.

He'd noticed Bob Butler watching the match intently from the terrace outside on the way in, and found the clubhouse virtually abandoned. Whilst it was so quiet, he took the opportunity to have an unobstructed, and peaceful, nosey around.

He found the changing rooms, door open, deserted - and with a variety of trousers, club ties - and shirts, hanging from the pegs.

He next found the gents and took an impromptu comfort-break - *well they were free, they won't be at lunch - and if queues can be avoided...*

He washed his hands, bypassed the ladies - and next found the storeroom, again open and deserted.

He was just about to stick his head in another room when he heard the sound of two ladies talking inside. The journalistic instinct kicked in, so he paused for a second quietly outside the door in case there was anything of interest to help the day-job:

'I'm sorry Rebecca!'

A watery-eyed Rebecca Chapman shook her head and looked her in the eye:

'Don't'

Deborah Knowles put her hand gently on the other woman's upper arm, but Rebecca Chapman swatted it straight off with her hand, causing it to smart a little:

'Just leave me alone, alright?'

'I mean it Rebecca!'

Rebecca Chapman raised her voice:

'LOOK. He was nothing to do with me anymore...and from all accounts - he was nothing to do with you either!'

Deborah Knowles jaw fell open:

Rebecca could not tell if this was genuinely news to her or not. Maybe she was just shocked that somebody had said to her face - what others must now be thinking to themselves? She must have seen the newspaper reports - surely?...maybe she was in denial??

'And what's that supposed to mean??'

A spiteful and snarling forced smile spread across the other's face:

'Oh didn't you know??...oh you poor thing! Yes, he'd traded you in for a *much* younger and more beautiful model already!'

Deborah Knowles sobbed as Rebecca Chapman shook her head again - *she actually pitied the other woman...she'd been there herself of course!*

There was a gentle knock on the door - accompanied by a simultaneous *ahem* cough, as a gentleman with sandy-coloured hair, and wearing oval-shaped spectacles stepped into the room. He held an empty plastic pint glass in one hand - and a Panama cricket hat in the other.

Davieson stepped into a kitchen full of cling film-wrapped plates of sandwiches, sausage rolls, pork pie and *French Fancy* sponge cakes. A stainless steel tea urn steamed away in the corner of the room.

'Hello, ladies. I was wondering if I might speak to one or both of you about Peter Chapman? You know, what he was like? How he'll be missed??...That sort of thing'

Rebecca Chapman folded her arms and stormed out of the room. In doing so, she accidentally trod on Davieson's right foot as she brushed past him. It hurt more than he thought it would but she didn't apologise or even acknowledge the incident!

'You'll have to speak to her about that one I'm afraid!' she yelled back - and slammed the door behind her...

***

The afternoon's play had commenced.

He passed Alan Chambers in deep conversation with John Middleton and an emotional Rebecca

Chapman, on the way back out to the field of play. He nodded briefly at Alan.

He'd catch up with them some other time.

As he snaked his way through the spectators - carefully chaperoning his beer, he almost collided with a gentleman coming in the opposite direction. The gentleman had a flat cap on his head that was pulled so far down at the peak, that he had likely had no sight of Davieson approaching - or anyone else for that matter until he was practically upon them.

Davieson quickly sidestepped the man, allowing his plastic glass to roll with the motion and (despite the sudden change of direction) keep its prized contents safely suspended within.

'Sorry' the man apologised, briefly looking up from beneath the peak of the cap and looking Davieson in the eye.

'Don't mention it...I didn't spill a drop'

The man walked on.

Davieson looked back over his shoulder, set his beer down - and fumbled in his blazer. He produced one of the archive newspaper clippings that he had been carrying around with him ever since his story ran, and checked it again. He nodded, satisfied:

Well well well. Geoffrey Wright back here where he might have been able to prevent ALL that had later followed, had he taken a more firm hold of affairs that wretched day!

He put the *Latchfords'* clipping back in his pocket, retrieved his beer, and returned to his deckchair to enjoy the play, and further people-watching.

At the end of the match - a fine *Upper Woodleigh* victory, wrapped up when Danny Johnson had managed to hold on to a difficult catch that he shouldn't have been able to get anyway near - Craig Ellsmere led his victorious team off the field of play, warmly patting the back of the *man-of-the-match*.

He had filled big boots again...in fact, they hadn't missed *him* at all - and the young starlet had done very well again...

***

Back at home, Davieson thought that he would make a quick call before pouring himself a liberal glass of malt and relaxing for the evening.

He phoned *Police Headquarters*.

'Can I speak with Chief Inspector Kent please?'

'Who's calling please?'

'Merv Davieson'

'Does he know what it's regarding please?'

'He does yes - I was with him earlier today'

'One moment please'

Davieson lifted down a boxed bottle of a 12-year-old *Speyside* malt whilst he waited.

'Davieson!'

'Good evening Chief Inspector"

'Good evening. What can I do for you?'

'I know you had to shoot off with Jones...but I thought I'd let you know that *Upper Woodleigh* won Chief Inspector'

'Oh...they did?? Well thank you Davieson'

Kent was decidedly underwhelmed - *he had thought Davieson was on to something.*

There was a brief pause:

'Errr - whilst you're on Chief Inspector....'

Kent smiled:

'Yes??'

'I wondered what the groundsman had to speak to you about? *Anything newsworthy??*...publishable or otherwise!'

'Well, it was certainly interesting Davieson. He says that he had various items stolen or moved from his storeroom at the pavilion'

'Items?? What type of items?'

'Well his *Wellington b*oots'

Davieson recalled the footprint in Peter Chapman's kitchen.

'And??'

'His gardening gloves'

Davieson had by now, grabbed his notepad, and was scribbling down as Kent spoke.

'Go on'

'His shovel'

Davieson let out a long low contemplative whistle.

'Yes - we had a similar reaction ourselves, Davieson'

'Was there more?'

'Oh yes...his screwdriver'

'Ok'

'...and his *turf aerating* fork!'

'His what??'

'It's a *groundsman* thing Davieson. The important bit you'll be interested in...is that it's a 3-pronged fork with 7" long solid tines'

Davieson let out another long low whistle. He was painting a picture in his head, and already mulling over possibilities. He was silent for some time.

'You still there Davieson??'

'Sorry - I am Chief Inspector. I was just wondering if he was missing any pliers??'

'Pliers??'

'Yes'

'He didn't say so'

'Well did you ask?'

'Errr no. We didn't'

'Well he may not have come to use them again yet Chief Inspector - so he may not (as yet) know if he's missing any'

'What are you thinking Davieson??'

'The tooth Chief Inspector - the tooth'

'The tooth??'

'Yes. The rest of the items read like a handy (and ready-made) murder, mutilation - and disposal kit you see. But the tooth extraction - well...'

Chapter Thirty-Five

They again pulled up opposite an untidy and unkempt front garden, even more overgrown than it had been on their previous visit.

It was the height of the growing season - the weeds were taking an ever more firmer hold on things...and there had evidently been zero maintenance, or tidying, carried out in the period between their two visits.

They strode smartly up the driveway.

Chief Inspector Kent banged the door, took a good three lengthy paces backwards to rejoin Sergeant Jones where he had just deposited him - and waited patiently.

In due course, the former wicketkeeper of *Upper Woodleigh Cricket Club* opened his front door to the world once again and the now-familiar noxious odour quickly greeted them. *The man must have had kippers again for his breakfast - did he ever eat anything else??* Kent was beginning to wonder. It was again the predominant stench, amongst a toxic combination of collective stenches!

Fortunately, Kent had timed the opening so that he could enjoy a last lungful of reasonably fresh air, just prior to the seal on Roger Lenton's abode being broken. He decided that he would subsequently breathe through his mouth until he had completed what he had come here to do!

'Mr. Lenton'

The homeowner squinted in the bright sunshine as his pupils constricted. He rubbed a crusted sleep-filled eye, and recognised his visitors:

'Oh, hello'

The Chief Inspector looked straight down at Roger Lenton's feet. They were shod in a pair of wrinkled cotton socks that had seen better days, and fraying and holey carpet slippers. The slippers themselves were further tarnished with an array of unidentifiable stains.

Through one of these holes, could be seen one of Roger's gnarled (and blackened) toenails protruding out of a corresponding hole in the sock beneath it - like part of a crumbling mummy's corpse, poking out of perished ancient bandages.

Kent shook his head silently, in further continued disgust at this *wretch of a man* the case had put his way, and then finally looked back up at him:

'This the only footwear you own sir?'

Roger Lenton followed the tall policeman's gaze and looked down at his own feet. He shook his head:

'No of course not - I've got some shoes!'

'Good! May we see a pair then please?...preferably some cleaner ones!'

He looked confused:

'I'm not sure what this is about, but yes I'll fetch you a pair'

'Please do....we'll, errr - wait outside!'

As Roger Lenton disappeared along his hall, to locate a pair of shoes, Kent took the opportunity to stride a few paces back down the driveway in the direction of the road and replenish the air in his lungs.

Jones sniggered as Kent let out a breath that he had been holding for longer than he should. The veins had noticeably bulged in his superior officer's temples briefly, and a flush of colour had consequently swept across the Chief Inspector's cheeks.

A few deep breaths later, and Kent had regained his normal colour and felt suitably reoxygenated by the time that Roger Lenton had returned balancing a scuffed exhibit in each hand.

He wandered over and let Roger Lenton leave them hanging there. Without physically touching them himself, he closed one eye, lowered his head and peered inside with the other eye.

They were size elevens.

'Bag them please Jones'

'Righto sir'

Kent leant in close to Jones and raised a hand over his mouth to quietly whisper in the latter's ear:

'He probably found those' he joked: 'He probably takes a size ten or twelve if he took the time to actually crawl out of his hovel and buy a pair!!'

Jones didn't know whether to laugh with the Chief Inspector or not!

'I wouldn't know that sir' he whispered back.

'I'll give you a receipt for these now Mr. Lenton, and we'll have them back with you as soon as we can'

He thrust some paperwork at Roger Lenton, handed him a cheap biro - and asked him to sign on a dotted line, indicated by an authoritative prodding finger. The latter signed it somewhat half-heartedly and handed both items back. The tall policeman briefly gave the pen the once-over, wiped it on his used handkerchief - and returned it to his coat pocket.

Kent nodded to Jones, and without saying a word to each other, the two policemen wheeled around to make their departure, leaving Roger Lenton looking somewhat flabbergasted on his doorstep:

'But they're my shoes Chief Inspector!'

Kent halted and spun around:

'Going out, are we sir?'

Roger Lenton shrugged. *That was highly unlikely if he was perfectly honest about it*:

'Well no, but...'

'Then you won't be needing them, sir! Good day...'

***

The drive was empty.

Was he out?? He'd try anyway.

He rapped the door and smiled when Alan Chambers opened it.

'Hello again'

The Welshman beamed, and the smile was returned.

'Ah hello - please do come in'

'Thank you, sir'

Davieson stepped inside and rubbed his shoes on the doormat. He looked up at his host:

'Firstly I must apologise to you'

'*Apologise??*'

'Yes. The scorecard you so kindly loaned me...well I can't return it I'm afraid'

Alan Chambers looked confused and scratched his head. He looked like he was trying hard to recall it:

'Oh, that - yes...lost it have you??'

Davieson shook his head:

'No I haven't lost it, but the, errr - police wanted to take custody of it, so I had to give it up...they were very adamant'

The secretary of *Upper Woodleigh Cricket Club* nodded:

'Ah...I understand. Not to worry - no doubt they'll return it for our archives when they've finished with it'

'I'm sure they will sir. I'm sure they will'

Alan Chambers shut the front door:

'Anyway, this way'

He pointed and they walked through to the lounge. Davieson spoke again:

'Secondly Mr. Chambers, I didn't get a chance to catch up with you at the match - but I wanted to ask your opinion as to who might have *had it in* for Peter Chapman?'

The secretary huffed:

'Who wouldn't, you might more easily ask!'

Davieson smiled:

'Like that is is?'

'It is indeed. Well, I'll make us a drink, and then I'll let you know how I see it. *Tea??*'

'Tea would be lovely thanks'

The journalist sat down on the sofa, and Alan Chambers disappeared into his kitchen to make them both tea, leaving the Welshman alone. The latter cast his eye around the room.

He spotted a bookshelf and darted straight over to it. He quickly perused the thicker volumes whilst he had the opportunity and found a Bible. There was a bookmark placed inside it.

He stood still, and first checked that he could still hear Alan Chambers busy in his kitchen.

He sounded busy, so Davieson lifted it down carefully, and noted where the bookmark had been placed.

It was open at Ephesians Chapter 6. He briefly referred to the biblical notes he had previously made, shook his head - and quickly returned it to his proper place.

He was back on the sofa when Alan Chambers returned with the tea and handed him a mug.

'Thank you. So those that, errr - *had it in* for Peter??'

The secretary raised his eyebrows, as Davieson produced his notepad and biro:

'Well take his wife Rebecca (they're separated now) for starters. Happily married (they seemed), and a lovely lady too - well, he's only gone and ditched her, and taken up with the other lady who works alongside her to provide our renowned club teas...Deborah Knowles!'

Davieson tutted as Alan Chambers continued:

'Yes taken it very badly she has...and moved back in with her parents I believe. It gets worse too!'

'Go on'

'Deborah Knowles is also a player's wife so *Andrew Knowles* has taken this badly too. In fact, he confronted Peter about it in the lounge bar, after the players had been practising in the nets the other Thursday night.

A very unsavoury episode. Yes - there was glass and beer flying everywhere, and other players had to pull the pair of them apart...not before Andrew had been hurt quite badly, and felled by a punch to the face, I might add!

Poor old Bob had to stay up half the night, mopping up spilt beer, and sweeping up broken glass - whilst the rest of us were back home and tucked up in bed. He's a volunteer (bless him) like the rest of us, so he shouldn't have to put up with that sort of thing.

Bob's wanted him barred for some time, but the committee has welcomed the money Peter Chapman spent behind the bar...so we've reluctantly tolerated him'

The Welshman scribbled furiously:

'And can I just clarify which Thursday please?'

'It was the one just before the previous home game - the first game that Peter Chapman didn't play in... although we didn't know the reason why he wasn't there then of course'

'No, of course not'

'And Andrew isn't the only player he's come to blows with too of late!'

'Oh??'

'No - poor old Danny Johnson...not our safest pair of hands at *Upper Woodleigh* I might add, had the misfortune to drop catches Peter had set up, *three times* in the same match, just the last time they played together.

Well, Peter Chapman was super-competitive...always has been. He obviously felt that all his hard work (I'm talking about his bowling) was being undone by Danny's incompetence, of course. Most would just accept the bad luck...we are an amateur side after all, but no - Peter verbally abused him for the first two dropped catches...then absolutely flipped his lid at the third!'

'What did he do then exactly?'

'Well, he marched straight over to Danny (mid-over this was), halting the game, to remonstrate with him.

He shouts in his face *YOU DID THAT DELIBERATELY!*

Next thing we know, he's got poor old Danny pinned to the deck with his fingers clamped around his throat vice-like. Again our other players had to separate the two of them. Very embarrassing for the club too - it resulted in our very first fine by the district league in fact!'

Alan Chambers took a sip of his tea.

'*Did* Danny drop him deliberately??'

The secretary put his tea back down:

'Well, I hadn't thought of it like that to tell you the truth. I don't *think so*...but I couldn't be positive on the matter. Say...you're not going to quote me on all of this are you??'

'Of course not sir - I'll wrap it all up as *Peter Chapman (by all accounts) was not particularly popular with the locals!* That ok??'

'Yes, that'd be fine...just I have to see and work with these people you understand?'

'I do sir - I do indeed. So, what did the other players think of Peter?'

'Well team-mates' didn't like him - and neither did our opponents. You hear of *sledging* your opponents now and then...but not your own side too!

It's Craig I always felt most sorry for though. Craig often had a harder time than the rest of them...Craig Ellsmere - our 1st XI Captain I should add. Craig ought to have been in charge in terms of team selection, and out on the field of play...you know, fielding positions, who should bowl the next over and such like, but no - Peter constantly strove to undermine him'

'In what way??'

'Just endlessly challenging his authority. Peter would think he always knew best, and would bore him with his *I had trials for the county you know?* line.

We were *all* sick and tired of hearing that one! We knew he was good, we knew he'd had trials for the county...but we didn't need it constantly ramming down our throats!

Rumour has it, of course - that the county would have signed him if he hadn't have had such a high opinion of himself...they thought he'd be bad for dressing room morale.

Yes, he had many a *run-in* with Craig'

'And the old nasty accident that there was here at *Upper Woodleigh*...did that taint his standing with others??'

'Oh yes! So then there's poor old Roger of course. He's never been the same since...a shadow of his former self!

The episode completely shattered his confidence, and so we don't see him anymore at the club...I don't think anyone does, full stop, to be fair. No, he doesn't venture outside anymore. It's such a shame'

'Did the accident annoy anyone *other* than Roger?'

'Oh, for sure - yes'

'Anyone in particular??'

'Well, Peter's attitude was appalling that day too. Bullying our opponents' Captain, and bullying the Umpire himself (would you believe it) too? He was dreadful!

Their Captain wanted the game calling off as the light deteriorated, but Peter got right in his face, invading his personal space...and the Umpire's too, ranting away like a mad man. I imagine that neither of them put Peter Chapman on their Christmas Card list that day!'

'And players-aside, what about non-paying officials? What did they think about him here?'

'Well Ted - our groundsman, he's had many a practical joke played on him by Peter over the years'

'What kind of jokes?'

'Pinching his stuff, you know??'

'*His stuff??*'

'Yes, clothes and such like'

'Any clothing items in particular?'

'I think missing socks were Peter's favourite prank...trousers too!'

Davieson grinned sympathetically.

'And what about your Chairman? What did John Middleton think of him?

'*John??* Wait a minute'

He walked over to his refrigerator and removed a letter that was affixed to it with a fridge magnet. He first held it against his chest so that the Welshman could only see the blank reverse.

'Well, John had a hard time of it...continually really, trying to remain diplomatic and intervening when he had to. It would be John who both tried to calm Bob down if there was an incident in the bar, and have the quiet word with Peter about his conduct.

I believe the latter largely fell on deaf ears, so a thankless task really, and not a job I would have wanted myself!'

Alan Chambers remained silent for a moment or too, appearing to contemplate the paper pinned to his chest. He turned it around and walked towards the journalist:

'Have you, errr - seen this whilst you've been researching your newspaper coverage??'

He handed Davieson the extraordinary committee meeting summons they'd all received...

Chapter Thirty-Six

'MR. ELLIS!'

Ted Ellis turned his head, switched off the engine, and brought the motorised mower to a stop - the Chief Inspector's bellow being of sufficient volume to attract his attention over the sound of the mower's oppressive chugging motor. He removed a set of soft foam earplugs from either side of his head and placed them in his overalls' pocket:

'Sorry - didn't see you there'

'That's quite alright, sir - that's a noisy piece of machinery you have there...may we have a word please?'

Kent noted that he was decked out in bright shiny new *Wellington* boots. There was not a speck of dirt to be found upon them, and the sun dazzled blindingly off their surface.

'Sure'

'We'd like to see the storeroom here please Mr. Ellis...your *den* as you term it'

Ted Ellis nodded:

'Ok. Well, we better head inside then...I could do with a cuppa anyway'

The tall policeman smiled:

'That sounds most agreeable sir'

Kent, Ted Ellis and Sergeant Jones walked three abreast towards *Upper Woodleigh Cricket Club's* pavilion.

They stopped off en route to the storeroom, to order three teas from Bob Butler, who was busying himself in the lounge bar. The latter appeared to be lifting various photographs down from the walls of the bar and stacking them in a large empty cardboard box. He wasn't being particularly gentle with the stacking!

The removal was leaving an assortment of bold impressions, on walls that had faded over time...under the combined (and relentless) forces of direct sunlight, cobwebs - and house dust. Shadow images now remained, where the framed photographs had formerly hung, and Kent thought it unsightly...*the club would certainly need to redecorate!*

He kept his thoughts to himself as three teas were duly deposited on the bar counter, and the barman eyed his three customers keenly.

'Right then sir...let's see this storeroom then please'

Ted collected one of the teas, nodded to Bob Butler without speaking - and set off:

'This way then gentlemen'

They followed the groundsman through the pavilion, along a corridor - and into the storeroom, the door was propped wide open with a door wedge.

The Chief Inspector surveyed the scene before him:

'So this is where the items went missing from? Is that right sir??'

Ted nodded:

'That's right'

Kent looked down at Ted's feet:

'And I take it these boots are new then, and that the originals have not turned up?'

'That's right - I only picked these new boots up recently. You haven't traced them then??'

'I'm afraid not sir'

'Not to worry. These aren't as comfortable as the old boots yet...but they do the job you know!'

'I'm sure they do sir. Anyway - have you got a pair of pliers in here Mr. Ellis?'

'Sure - they're in my toolbox'

'May we see them please sir?'

'Of course. Follow me'

The two policemen followed the groundsman over to a corner of the room. The latter bent down and picked up a battered (but sturdy) grey metal toolbox, set it down on the seat of a chair - and flipped open its lid.

He rummaged around plentiful contents, and gradually lifted out a variety of spanners, drill bits, clear plastic bags full of nuts and bolts, similar bags of nails, a bag of screws, a chisel - and a lump hammer.

Ted Ellis had placed all these items in a heap at the side of the chair. He straightened his back, removed a cloth cap from his head - and scratched his head.

'I'm sorry but they're not here. I may have mislaid them'

'Well, when did you last use them?'

'I don't recall sorry. I tend to mainly only use them to remove stubborn nails and tacks from our wooden noticeboards outside. That's where we display posters and such like, to keep residents and spectators up to date with club news, fixtures and social functions'

'You didn't take it round to Peter Chapman's place recently by any chance did you sir??'

Kent was *chancing his arm*. It back-fired, and immediately put Ted Ellis on the defensive:

'No comment'

'I see sir. Well, we're going to need a key for this storeroom, and it's out-of-bounds until further notice!'

'But I haven't finished mowing yet...and then I need to repair divots and get litter picking. The footfall was considerable at the weekend's game - a record attendance here in fact, and the ground has taken a right old battering. You should see the amount of rubbish that was discarded too! It's blowing about all over the place...well that rubbish that hasn't been trodden firmly into the earth that is...I stood in grated cheese and beetroot earlier, would you believe!'

Ted Ellis swung a leg forward, grabbed the underneath of his thigh for support - and showed the two policemen the sole of his boot.

There was a piece of beetroot wedged firmly in the tread.

If you hadn't have seen it for yourself, then you never would have believed that such shiny new boots could somehow be sullied in such a way thought Kent.

Both policemen suppressed a smirk.

'I'm sorry sir'

He wasn't!:

'...Now the key please!'

He didn't look happy, but Ted Ellis stomped across the storeroom in a huff and retrieved his set of keys which we're hanging in the door. He walked back over to Kent - who held his hand out authoritatively, and placed the bunch of keys down petulantly in the Chief Inspector's palms.

'Thank you, sir. We'll see ourselves out'

Ted reluctantly filed out of his domain, forlornly looking back over his shoulder at the two policemen as he left.

They waited until he was out of the room:

'Right then Jones - we need this place dusting for fingerprints from top to bottom'

'Righto Chief Inspector'

'...And station a man on the door there - it's been far too much of a free-for-all in here until now!...'

***

'Hello John...we spoke on the telephone'

'Errr??'

The Chairman of *Upper Woodleigh Cricket Club* looked a little vacant as he stood in his doorway facing the stranger who had just addressed him.

'Davieson...Merv Davieson - *The Morning Chronicle*'

'Ah yes - of course. Please do come in'

He pointed a welcoming arm immediately behind him and Davieson followed him into the house.

The Chairman continued:

'I understand now of course, why you were writing a newspaper article on our beloved cricket club!'

'...Well, why it's taking the course it's now following at least' admitted Davieson.

'Oh come on - you knew full well what you were really interested in all along. It had *nothing* to do with our fine and extensive history'

The Chairman smiled at him.

'You misunderstand me, sir. What I meant is that yes...I admit that I did know about Roger - and his dreadful accident. I had no prior knowledge of Peter Chapman though'

John Middleton laughed:

'Apologies, I'm having a bit of fun with you. I actually don't mind in the slightest. You're discreet in your approach (I'll give you that) - and you write very very well. Unfortunately, many of your peers don't write so well, however - utter rubbish what some of them have reported, and not in keeping with how we like things here at *Upper Woodleigh*'

The Welshman blushed:

'Thank you, sir. How do you like things here at *Upper Woodleigh*??'

'Well it's a beautiful game - and a game for gentlemen. It does not belong in the small inches of the gutter press!'

'Quite' agreed Davieson.

'Well I was just making tea - care for some?'

'That'd be lovely thanks'

Unless absolutely pushed for time, experience had taught Davieson to accept every invitation going, that would necessitate having to spend more time with his intended interviewee. Acceptance would generally lead to fuller facts, snippets he might not otherwise uncover - and a more rounded storyline for his readers.

'Take a seat, I won't be a moment'

Davieson sat himself down.

True to his word, the Chairman was back in a minute or two, rattling two steaming china teacups and teaspoons in their respective saucers. It had been just time enough for the Welshman to swiftly open a Bible he had spotted in John Middleton's lounge. A page corner had been turned over - and initially looked promising...but ultimately proved disappointing. It was turned over at a page within the *wrong Gospel*.

Davieson half rose from his seat and took the cup and saucer handed to him:

'Smashing, thank you. I errr watched the game on Saturday...I must say that I found the brief eulogy you gave for Peter Chapman very moving sir'

Did John Middleton hesitate? Had the statement caused him to briefly petrify and stop him dead in his tracks? Whatever the effect - a wave of colour flushed his cheeks.

'Errr, thank you'

'...Still, this all must be tarnishing the good name *Upper Woodleigh Cricket Club* had I guess?'

John Middleton was about to take a sip of his tea but instead clattered his teacup down in the saucer:

'Damn right it is man!'

'That's a real shame. It was not so long ago that your Secretary, Alan, was showing me a vast array of memorabilia, and a splendid trophy cabinet...you must have been the envy of the district league?'

'Oh we were...still will be if I have my way!'

'*Your way??*'

'...Figure of speech sorry'

'There must be something you could do though?? As Chairman of your cricket club, you're an influential man Mr. Middleton...have you mobilised your committee? - got them helping restore your fine reputation??'

'Have you been speaking to any of them?'

With immaculate timing, Davieson evasively took the opportunity to try his tea. He feigned being unable to respond - due to a mouthful of hot tea, and the ploy worked like clockwork.

'Nevermind. No - as *the man at the helm*, I feel that I'm largely responsible for that'

'You don't think that any of the others might have thought they were restoring this reputation by errr....*getting rid* of Peter Chapman? He'd brought the club into disrepute on a number of occasions I hear!'

'Well, I wouldn't mobilise action of that nature - if that's what you're suggesting!'

'I didn't suggest that sir'

'You think I'd sit down at the head of a committee table, and ask the committee if *any of them would kindly volunteer and get rid of Peter for us??*'

'Again, I didn't suggest that sir'

'To do such a thing publicly would incriminate myself...I could be accused of abetting!'

John Middleton was becoming more animated (and red-faced) by the minute.

'I'm not accusing you of anything Mr. Middleton...I'm not the police remember'

John Middleton was unsure if he should find that reassuring or not.

'When did the committee last meet anyway?'

He calmed a little:

'Errr, Wednesday evening'

'*Wednesday?*'

Davieson nodded gently:

'...And what did you discuss?'

'I don't recall sorry'

'*You don't recall??*'

'No...it's been a busy week!'

There was a lengthy silence followed, that verged on the uncomfortable.

Davieson smiled:

'Well nevermind Mr. Middleton, I know you're a busy man - I won't keep you further and thank you for the cuppa'

He stood up to leave.

'No problem - my pleasure...I'll show you out'

As John Middleton showed him out, the Welshman timed his steps back to the door, so that he casually planted a foot next to a pair of men's shoes he had observed just inside the hall, as he had stepped in earlier.

He had noted two pairs lying there. One obviously footwear belonging to John Middleton - the other, equally apparent, belonging to the lady of the house - Mrs. Middleton.

John Middleton was completely oblivious to the staged experiment, but Davieson had his answer:

They were too small...

Chapter Thirty-Seven

There was a knock on Chief Inspector Kent's door at *Police Headquarters*.

'Come in'

'Hello, sir. We got the results of the fingerprinting exercise undertaken at the cricket pavilion'

'Excellent!'

Kent rose expectantly and near-snatched the report from his colleague's hand.

He skim-read the detail and an executive summary:

A plethora of fingerprints positively identified as those of Ted Ellis. Additionally, several other sets of prints have been successfully attributed to other individuals connected with Upper Woodleigh Cricket Club - those who have been formally interviewed and had their prints taken during investigations to date, into the recent double-murders. Otherwise, fingerprints, fingerprints - and fingerprints on fingerprints, decorate the storeroom from head to foot! Several weeks work would therefore, be necessary to try and make any meaningful headway into identifying these remaining prints. This could only be progressed if adequate resource could be made available of course, and we await your further instruction.

'Yes, thank you sergeant - that'll be all'
The Chief Inspector did not seem pleased!
'I wonder if our journalist friend is getting on any better than we appear to be here??'
He decided to phone the offices of *The Morning Chronicle*:
'Merv Davieson please'
'Who shall I say is calling please?' came an unfamiliar voice at the other end.
'Chief Inspector Kent'
'Putting you through now sir'
They were soon connected.
'Davieson'
'Hello, Chief Inspector. How is your investigation progressing?'
'Well, that's exactly why I'm phoning you Davieson. We seem to have hit a definite bottleneck, and so the case appears to be grinding to a near standstill'
'Oh??'
'Yes, on the one hand, it looks fairly conclusive now, that our murderer had kitted themself out with eveything they needed to commit these heinous and barbaric acts of mutilation and murder, from the storeroom at *Upper Woodleigh Cricket Club* pavilion'

'But??'

'But the trouble is Davieson, that *every man and his dog* would have appeared to have been in the storeroom at one time or another. It's got a lock on the door alright. It's got a key for the lock too - but do they use it?...do they...'

'...Yes it was open when I popped my head in there too'

'You were in the storeroom??'

'Yes'

'When was this?'

'Oh, on the day of the cricket match...you'd taken the groundsman back to *Police Headquarters* to make a statement, and I'd headed inside the pavilion for a pint...got myself lost in there!'

'Oh, I see. Well we now subsequently need to sift through a multitude of prints to try and progress things further and find out who walked in there, helped themselves to the items - and made off with them, never to be seen again'

'So have you any theories, Chief Inspector, as to who may have done just that, and waltzed out with a turf fork, screwdriver, pair of boots and so on?'

'I haven't Davieson - it could have been anyone!'

'...Well that's one (possibly laborious) angle of investigation you could take I guess'

Chief Inspector Kent was interested in Davieson's words:

'There's another??'

'I may be speaking out of turn'

'Don't worry about that Davieson - I'm more than open to suggestions at this stage of the investigation'

'Well. Have you considered (by chance) that Ted Ellis may have reported these items missing to throw yourselves off guard...off the scent if you like, and keep the investigation a good distance from himself?'

'I hadn't, no'

'Well I had considered, and found myself on the day of the cricket match, that pretty much anyone could get into the storeroom...particularly on a match day when greater numbers are busying about'

'Ok'

'Carrying a turf fork and shovel around with you, however, would be somewhat conspicuous, and attract undue attention...particularly if it did not ordinarily belong to you, or be *tools of the trade* that you would reasonably be expected to use and carry whilst undertaking your normal duties'

'So??'

'So the one person possibly carrying all these items around, that no one would bat an eyelid at...'

'...Would be the groundsman!'

'Would be the groundsman, yes...'

Chapter Thirty-Eight

The suited man pulled off the drive and drove away.

Davieson waited until the car was safely out of sight, stepped out of his own car - and walked up the drive. He gently rapped the front door.

'Hello. Rebecca Chapman said I had to ask you about what Peter Chapman was like and how he'll be missed!'

Deborah Knowles looked blankly at the Welshman.

The latter beamed back at her expectantly.

She coloured scarlet and forced a polite smile:

'Oh, that!'

'Yes I think I caught you two at a bad moment at the cricket match'

'Something like that' she replied.

'So is it a better time now madam??'

'I guess so - you're the press right?'

'That's right madam...Merv Davieson - *The Morning Chronicle*'

'Come in'

'Thank you, madam'

Davieson wiped his shoes several times on the doormat, glancing briefly at a man's pair of shoes lying next to the mat and followed Deborah Knowles into her kitchen, where the latter offered him a chair at the kitchen table. She did not offer him a drink...he didn't push it and proceeded to produce a notepad and biro from his blazer pocket.

The Welshman tutted and looked around the kitchen a little helplessly. There was a solitary sheet left in his notepad:

'Sorry, you haven't got a hard book I could lean on have you please?'

'Sure. My bookcase is in the lounge – let's move through to there'

'Oh, ok'

He followed her through to the lounge and hovered over her shoulder whilst Deborah Knowles selected a suitable hard-backed leaning aid.

She handed him a volume of poetry.

'Thank you – that's great. So what *was* Peter like madam?'

He took the top off his biro and poised ready to scribble.

She let out a sigh:

'Well I know he wasn't everyone's cup of tea, but for me - well...I kind of liked him'

'So why did you like him then madam? - when others weren't such a fan. What did you see in him that others didn't'

She blushed again.

'Well, I admit that I'd always found Peter handsome and had had a soft spot for him for a while. He was the star of the First XI by all accounts, and I just couldn't help myself giving him a friendly smile if it happened to be me who topped his teacup up at a break in play. Call it fanciful hero-worship if you like.

Well, eventually he started giving me a discrete wink or two when he and the players filed into the pavilion - right with Rebecca stood beside me too! I don't think she ever caught him doing that...and I guess I felt flattered with the attention he was giving me. Things hadn't been brilliant between myself and my husband Andrew for some time before that you see'

'I see' said Davieson.

'So things developed and in what seemed like no time at all we were having an affair'

'I see' said Davieson again.

'You have to understand that I was in a difficult - and surreal situation!'

'*Surreal*??'

'Yes, well Rebecca and I - we'd been such good friends you see, working side by side in the cricket club kitchens for many years making our famous cricket teas and lunches.

Well, I guess things changed at home somewhat, and when Rebecca first got wind of the suspicion that Peter might be having an affair...she does no more than confide in me!'

Davieson raised his eyebrows. Deborah Knowles continued her recollection:

'Well I didn't know where to look, did I?

She then asked me for advice as to what I thought she should do.

She was trembling and I could tell she was upset...she sounded proper vindictive too!'

'Oh yeah?'

'Yes, I can see her now - gritting her teeth, and hear her utter *If I can't have Peter - then nobody will!*'

'What did you do?'

'Well, I asked her what *she* was going to do?...I was worried for myself you see!'

'And what did she say?'

'Nothing'

'*Nothing??*'

'Yes, she just seemed to go into some kind of trance...lost in her thoughts'

'I see. And when did you see Peter Chapman last?'

'It would have been late June'

'Not since then??'

'No - it would have been the previous home fixture you see when I was making the teas with Rebecca'

'Ok'

'I did *try* and see him again'

'You did?'

'Yes, I went round to his house when Andrew slipped out of the house sulking one day. Andrew was sporting a black eye and his face was swollen something rotten'

'When was this?'

'It would have been Friday the 5th July. I remember Andrew had come back from his nets practice the night before with his shiner. I guess he hadn't been wearing a helmet!'

'So you were at Peter's?'

'Well, I didn't get to the house itself...I just turned around and came home'

'Why was that?'

'Well he had company'

Company??'

'Yes, there was some blue car parked up there...that young girl the police were trying to locate I imagine...'

Chapter Thirty-Nine

'Danny Johnson??'

'That's right'

'Terrific catch at the weekend sir!'

The mid-order batsman blushed and smiled:

'Thank you...I take it you were there?'

'I was indeed sir - fielding of the highest order...Errr, sorry - Merv Davieson..*The Morning Chronicle*'

'We're a bit small for your sports pages surely??...'

He quickly shook his head, briefly closed his eyes, snapped his fingers at Davieson - and laughed:

'Oh I realise now...sorry, stupid of me - the Peter stuff I guess?'

'That's right sir...the Peter Chapman *stuff*. May I, errr - have a word please?'

'Sure. Come in - would you like a drink?'

'A tea would be lovely thanks'

Danny Johnson sorted the teas. Davieson had a rudimentary search for a copy of a Bible whilst the former was busy - but it reaped no reward, and he took a seat.

Not that the presence or absence of a Bible would prove necessarily conclusive. He realised that it would be quite easy to dispose of such a book - after having taken murderous inspiration, should a suspect wish to then distance himself from his research material.

Household rubbish, village fetes, charity shop donation - or a simple bonfire in the back garden would all provide plentiful opportunities to innocently dispose of potential evidence without arousing suspicion.

Danny Johnson returned. Davieson took his mug of tea and continued the conversation:

'I understand that you haven't always held on to them quite as well as that one though??'

'The ball??...no, I've had a terrible spell in the field until Saturday's catch to be fair'

'Maybe you're a lot more relaxed now??' suggested Davieson cheekily.

'Now??' queried Danny Johnson.

'Yes...now that Peter Chapman has been murdered'

'I couldn't possibly comment...no offence like'

Did he briefly smile??

'That's quite alright sir...and none taken - but I understand that there had been an *altercation* and that Peter Chapman had recently pinned you to the ground, and humiliated you, in front of your team?'

'Says who?'

'I can't share that sir. Is it true?'

'Well what have you managed to establish?' retorted Danny.

'Well we speak to all sorts in our profession Mr. Johnson - but I'll be honest, this insight did feel like it was founded in the truth, and not mere idle gossip'

'Ok, so I admit I dropped one too many catches of his, and as a result, he went ballistic!...It ended up how you suggest'

'In front of all your team-mates too! That's several witnesses - and I guess that could leave you in a difficult position now that there's a murder investigation underway! Care to set the record state, and tell us how it is from your perspective...before others point the finger??'

Danny Johnson took the bait:

'Well he was a horrible character...so please don't paint him in a good light when you write your story up. The nation should know what a bully, and nasty piece of work, he really was!

Regarding our altercation - I couldn't do anything about this *public menace* at the time (he'd pinned me far too tightly to the deck and was shaking like a madman) but I was always taught to stand up to bullies and so I originally thought that I'd give him some of his own medicine at our next game'

'What did you do?'

'Nothing'

'Nothing??'

'No...he wasn't playing (I don't know why)'

Davieson already knew this but played dumb in the hope of obtaining new snippets of information and detail for his newspaper article.

'You'd no idea he wasn't playing?'

'No - he was usually the first name on the team sheet - was *old big head*'

'Anything else to set the record straight and help stifle gossip??'

Danny Johnson paced up and down the room twice, pondering with his hand on his chin. He stopped and looked at the Welsh journalist sat before him who had paid him this unexpected visit:

'I...*might* have been spotted near his property around the time of his death or the discovery of his body!'

'You *might*?? I don't understand!'

'Well I was marching there one evening to have it out with him'

'When exactly?'

'It would have been Friday 12th July, I later worked out'

'What did you do?'

'Again nothing'

'Did you manage to speak to him at least?'

'I didn't, no'

'How come??'

'I changed my plans at the last minute'

'Any reason?'

'Yes - some maniac nearly ran me down in the road. It shook me up something terrible, and I lost my bottle...I turned about and thought I'd have it out with him some other time'

'Didn't the driver see you?'

Danny Johnson looked awkward and embarrassed:

'Well, I was dressed in black...I wasn't entirely sure how things would pan out you see, and I thought I best try and blend into the shadows'

'You weren't entirely sure how things would pan out??...Do you mean you weren't entirely sure if you yourself would be running the poor man through with a fork?'

'A *fork??* That must have taken many blows...unless someone caught him right, and hit something vital'

Davieson ignored the question and incorrect assumption. *Did this man really think that Peter Chapman might have been murdered with table cutlery?? He shook his head.*

'What had you thought might happen then?...worse case scenario?...'

'I'm not sure - I was properly wound up...I'm not saying I would have killed the chap though!'

'No - I won't write that you might have killed the chap sir, so don't worry yourself there'

'Thank you'

'Out of interest...what size shoe do you take sir?'

'You're the second person who's asked that today!'

'Oh??'

'Yes, a policeman came knocking earlier, and asked the very same thing!'

'Did he now?'

The Welshman laughed.

'Yes...I'm one shoe down as a result!'

He fetched a lonely looking shoe that was in apparent need of a companion and dangled it in front of Davieson's eyes. He held a piece of paper in the other hand:

'He gave me a receipt mind...said I should get it back'

'And what size shoe do you take then?' pressed Davieson.

'I take an eleven' replied Danny Johnson...

Chapter Forty

They had both arranged a lift in order that they could enjoy a leisurely pint (or two) together and catch up on the case-cum-story.

For Davieson, a murder story that ran and ran was good for business and kept the *Chronicle's* readership hooked. They were buying the paper in huge numbers daily to keep abreast of developments.

For Chief Inspector Kent, it was the absolute opposite, as each day that passed without a firm arrest, charges being raised - or a voluntary confession, brought ever more difficult questions (largely surrounding his skills and capability to bring the case to a successful conclusion) from his superiors.

The investigation was being closely monitored in the highest quarters!

'So is there anything you can offer up to help me out Davieson? - anything you may have uncovered that folk aren't so keen to tell the police about?'

The Welshman took a sip of his pint and considered:

'Well did you hear about Peter Chapman's altercation with Danny Johnson?'

Kent stopped drinking - this was news to him:

'Danny Johnson being a member of the cricket team right??'

'That's right, yes'

'No I didn't I'm afraid - what have you been told?'

'Well I've only just learnt this myself, but when you seek comment for a newspaper article, many will often go at great length to point the finger...it was pointed out that Peter Chapman and Danny Johnson had been involved in a bust up recently.

I *hear* that Peter Chapman started it...and was quite violent with it too!

Mr. Johnson admits that he'd considered retribution - but says he errr...changed his mind'

'Did he sound convincing?'

'I'm not sure'

'Thank you Davieson - I'll look into it...anything else??'

'Yes - one other thing...I saw Geoffrey Wright at the cricket match'

'You did, did you?'

'I did...he was keeping a *very* low profile mind'

'Perhaps this historic accident didn't unsettle him quite as much as he had led us to believe then! I had thought it had put him off the game for life!!'

'Evidently not so, Chief Inspector'

'I'll admit that I've struggled to trust him from the start Davieson'

'Anyway, that's two from me!...any development on the official investigation side that I haven't written about?' chanced the experienced journalist.

'There is'

'The details...'

There was a brief pause. The Chief Inspector seemed to be debating whether to elaborate:

'So I've detained Ted Ellis!' he eventually dropped out, keen to gauge Davieson's reaction.

The Welshman nearly spat out his mouthful of beer back into his pint glass:

'You've arrested him?'

'...He's helping us with our enquiries!'

'Whatever!' replied Davieson with a wink - he felt a little guilty: 'Was this on the back of me suggesting that the most likely person to be carrying a shovel and fork around would be the club groundsman?'

The tall policeman nodded and bobbed his head left-right:

'After deliberation, that may have made my mind up' admitted Kent.

The journalist shook his head. He looked unsure in the strategy Kent was taking:

'I was probably generalising though Chief Inspector. I meant that if hypothesising that person x - may have carried out action y, relies on a fair stretch of the imagination - and verges on the edge of improbability...then maybe there's more of a straightforward solution to be had, and maybe that solution is staring us in the face!'

He took a long and satisfying gulp of his beer as the conversation stalled.

'Hmm' offered Kent, as he appeared to absorb what Davieson was saying thoughtfully.

'Let's just say that Ted Ellis did murder Peter Chapman though...what do you think now transpired?'

'Well that seems straightforward to me now Davieson'

'Go on??'

'Ted Ellis is fed up of Peter Chapman's practical jokes...I mean it's a form of bullying when sustained and not taken in good humour'

'Agreed there!'

'He gradually collates various equipment from his storeroom at the cricket pavilion - with murderous intent.

The cricket ground backing onto *Rowley Woods*, he has ample opportunity to spy on Peter Chapman's house at his leisure, from the lay-by on the other side of the woods, and work out all his regular comings and goings - his *Wellington* boots get a little muddy in doing so.

Research and preparation complete, he arrives at Peter Chapman's house, and the latter lets him in...it is Ted Ellis from the cricket club after all, so why not!

He murders him - leaves him dead on the kitchen floor, and when hunger takes him...he makes himself the famed cheese sandwich whilst he has the house to himself.

Suitably refreshed, he clears off and discreetly makes his way back through *Rowley Woods*'

Davieson nodded at length whilst Kent ran through his latest theory:

'Are you looking beyond Ted Ellis?'

'Well for completeness, I've also had Jones collate sample footwear from just about anyone I can think of that may have some bearing on the case.

I mean we've looked into your Bible angle too, Roger Lenton's was actually one of the finest examples we found - a splendid copy he has, and pretty much the cleanest thing we found in his house...and you may well be right re the source of our murderer's inspiration, but for me you can't beat plain hard evidence - give me a good old fashioned footprint over someone's reading habits any day!'

Davieson smiled politely:

'Boots and Bibles eh?'

'Is that one of your headlines??'

The Welshman laughed:

'Just thinking aloud Chief Inspector...I'd hope to come up with something more inspired than that!'

The tall policeman looked a little put out.

'So do you think we're right to pursue shoes Davieson?...Do you think the footprint was deliberately placed there to try and implicate Ted Ellis in the murder of Peter Chapman??'

Davieson puffed. He looked at Kent:

'Excuse the pun Chief Inspector...but *if I were in your shoes*...'

'Yes??'

Davieson had gone quiet - had he lost his train of thought??: 'Davieson??'

'Sorry - miles away, thinking about my newspaper story. Where was I??...yes, if I were in your shoes Chief Inspector, then I'd think about what we found at Peter Chapman's barn conversion'

'Well I've thought about that enough Davieson - can you be more specific??'

'Well what we found him wearing, his car, his house keys....and the cheese sandwich'

'R-i-g-h-t' said Kent slowly, as he tried to fathom out what Davieson was driving at...*he hadn't the foggiest*!

'Shall I tell you what I think?'

'Please do'

'Well take the clothes we found him in...they were the same clothes he'd only just left *Bathcombe Bay* in'

'So??'

'So I think that he was murdered *shortly* after he returned home to *Upper Woodleigh - before he' had chance to change into anything different in fact'*

'Ok - that sounds a fair assumption. His house keys??'

'His house was locked when we arrived right?'

Kent nodded.

'So you had to break the door down - there was no *prior* sign of forced entry'

'Agreed'

'So I think that either Peter Chapman let the killer in - somebody he knew...and just as you suggested he might for Ted Ellis'

There was a smile of self-satisfaction across the Chief Inspector's face.

'...or the killer got in the house somehow then locked the house back up as he/she left'

'O-k'

Kent didn't sound convinced, but wanted Davieson to tell him more:

'I forgot his lovely car sorry'

'His car, yes - well whilst we didn't see it at first, I believe you later found it safely locked away in his garage'

'That's right'

'He certainly took it to *Bathcombe Bay* to meet up with Jodi Fletcher, so I suggest that he drove it home and parked up with no idea he would shortly be confronted by his murderer'

'This cheese sandwich then??'

'The most important thing Chief Inspector!'

'Is it??'

'I think so'

'I'm not convinced Davieson'

'Humour me then Chief Inspector. Let's say you are going to murder Peter Chapman yourself'

'Ok' said Kent, suspiciously and cautiously.

'You somehow obtain entry to Peter Chapman's barn conversion'

'Ok'

'Peter Chapman arrives home...you're hiding somewhere in the shadows waiting for him. You take him by surprise before your presence there is discovered - and run him through with the errr...*turf aerating fork!*'

To add credibility to his narrative, Davieson deliberately included one of the established facts, in the supposition he was trying to relay to the sceptical Chief Inspector.

'He's now lying there dying in front of you, blood slowly spreading over his kitchen floor. Maybe this has shaken you up - maybe you can't quite believe that you have actually executed your murderous plan, and the cold reality of what you have done now hits home...you have committed a brutal murder!

You could be caught at any time of course! In the circumstances, you ought to get the hell out of there and remove yourself from the scene of the crime as fast as you can...but what do you do??'

He addressed the question directly at Kent.

'I don't know' admitted the Chief Inspector.

'Why it's obvious Chief Inspector...you make yourself a cheese sandwich before leaving!'

'Do I??'

'No of course not...I was being flippant sorry. No, you'd do no such thing'

'Yet we know *someone* helped themselves to a cheese sandwich'

'They did indeed Chief Inspector...and I still think that this was the murderer'

'I don't follow??'

'I think the murderer ate it *before* murdering Peter Chapman!'

'With him?...you know a meal for two??'

'No I don't think so - you said Peter Chapman hadn't consumed a cheese sandwich himself.

No I think the murderer had been in the house and lying in wait, for quite some time, and had been there for such a duration (maybe a couple of days or so) that hunger and thirst overcame them...the cheese sandwich and glass of water being a plain necessity - and not strange or odd post-killing behaviour from a laid-back murderer.

Maybe the killer had no idea that Peter Chapman had planned a late romantic liaison with Jodi

Fletcher at the coast - and had fully expected to find him at home when they first arrived...'

Chapter Forty-One

Davieson was back at *Folestree Parva*.

He hoped for the final time.

The police had long since had the blue car towed away, and so he was thus able to park in a convenient location for once!

'Excellent!' he said aloud to himself as he brought the car to a standstill.

He parked up, entered the post office - and found the postmaster himself on duty. It was Mandy's day off, and the post office was otherwise deserted.

'Hello again sir'

The postmaster smiled:

'You're that journalist right??'

'That's right sir. I guess you've been following the story. I was wondering if you had as yet, managed to recall who gave you that infamous package?'

The postmaster shook his head:

'I'm sorry I haven't I'm afraid'

Davieson reached inside his blazer pocket and showed the postmaster a photograph he had recently sourced:

'Was it this person by any chance??'

The postmaster looked at the photograph. He first squinted, as his eyes focussed - and then his eyes widened dramatically:

'Ah - yes of course...that cyclist!...'

Chapter Forty-Two

It was a glorious day.

Davieson parked his car at the foot of the sloping path - leaving the window ajar to let some air into the car whilst he left it there and proceeded to steadily climb the considerable hill that led up to the imposing parish church of *St. Catherine's* in *Upper Woodleigh*.

He thought he now had a very good idea as to exactly what had happened to Richard and Peter Chapman. He also thought he now understood how the murderer's mind had worked - and what motivation or inspiration lay behind the action the murderer had taken.

He hoped to have a better idea as to whether he was *barking up the wrong tree* or not here at *St. Catherine's*.

He crossed the churchyard, opened the aged outer door, and let himself into the porch. The cooler interior was most welcoming in the noon-day heat.

He surveyed the porch.

Between the inner and outer door, an array of church and parish notices were pinned to (and filled) a large cork noticeboard. Next to them, a pamphlet holder was stocked with paper copies of *A Brief History of St. Catherine's.*

Davieson ignored the pamphlets and studied the noticeboard in detail.

He had been there two or three minutes when a jovial and portly gentleman entered from outside.

He looked up as the door creaked open:

'Ah...Reverend Peters!'

'Errr, hello??'

'We met some time ago. Merv Davieson...*The Morning Chronicle*'

Reverend Peters scratched his head and then smiled:

'Of course, excuse my blank expression there - you must think terribly of me. I get forgetful sometimes nowadays...one sees so many faces at church, you see, that I sometimes struggle to put names to faces. *Davieson*...yes, I remember now. How are you?'

'Very well thanks. I've been back working in the area, and so I was just looking at what Bible study groups you have running here at *St. Catherine's*'

'Interested in joining are you?'

'I might be' lied Davieson. *He hoped the ultimate man in charge would forgive him the white lie!*

'Well we have a friendly Bible Study group here, that's for sure...plenty of characters too!'

'I'm sure you do Reverend. Do you meet here??'

'*Meet here*?? No - we meet at parishioners' houses. There's around half a dozen of the group regularly host our weekly meetings in their homes. I host one of the meetings myself at the vicarage in fact - and we each take it in turns to get the tea and biscuits in ready...it's all very friendly and relaxed'

They both laughed.

'Well you must tell me all about it, and who attends'

'More than happy to. I was just collecting some notes I left in the vestry, but if you'd care for a cuppa back at the vicarage, you can follow me home and I'll tell you when we next meet and more about our group'

'That'd be lovely thanks...'

Chapter Forty-Three

'Well, the body count appears to have slowed down!'

'It has indeed Davieson' agreed the tall policeman.

They were stood on the cricket boundary, gazing in the direction of the wicket and *Rowley Woods* beyond.

The Morning Chronicle's Chief Crime Reporter had asked Kent to join him there and explained on the telephone that he had something he needed to urgently discuss with the detective.

Kent had dropped everything and joined him at the cricket club as quickly as he could drive over there.

'I think I know why the rising body count has stopped too!

Yes, to quote a claim often made in print by *our lot* - I believe I have the full story Chief Inspector, and I believe (you'll be pleased to hear) that they'll be no more killing either'

'You do??'

'I do!

No doubt you also found - as I did Chief Inspector, that many people wanted Peter Chapman kicked out of *Upper Woodleigh Cricket Club*...or otherwise gotten rid of.

Rebecca Chapman (his wife) might want him dead for one, for taking up with Deborah Knowles. Deborah Knowles might want him dead herself if she got any inkling of the younger Jodi Fletcher now being on the scene.

Andrew Knowles might want him dead for stealing his wife - and to pick up where the pavilion bar fight left off when they were pulled apart by team-mates and club officials.

Danny Johnson had similar unfinished business to pick up again with Peter Chapman. His pride was wounded by the pinning to the deck episode.

Poor old Bob Butler was sick of the aggro in his bar, had wanted him barred on many occasions - and he'd had to clear up after the fight with Andrew Knowles.

John Middleton had seen his tight-knit family club, systematically pulled apart and destroyed by this womanising, arrogant bully.

Ted Ellis had been the butt of many a prank played on him by Peter Chapman. There were far too many of these and they were not welcome!

Craig Ellsmere had had many a run-in with Peter Chapman. The latter always demanding more overs - or challenging fielding positions. Constantly undermining his leadership and team selection.

Geoffrey Wright felt that he had been bullied by Peter Chapman, into continuing to play on when the failing light was making play dangerous.

David Heath - Captain of the opposing *Charnford* team, felt the same way, and that his protestations had been similarly railroaded by an aggressive and intimidating Peter.

And then there's poor old Roger of course, and where this whole episode began with the tragic loss of his eye'

'Yes, we've certainly had plenty of suspects to consider Davieson. It hasn't been at all straightforward from that respect'

The Welshman was silent for a moment, watching the tall policeman keenly.

'And yet I don't think any of these people committed these murders Chief Inspector'

Kent frowned:

'You don't??

'I don't - and I wanted to tell you why'

'*I'm all ears* Davieson'

'Well let me tell you how I arrived at this conclusion'

'Please do' encouraged Kent.

'I'll start, Chief Inspector, with our discovery of Peter Chapman's body.

As soon as we found Peter Chapman - lying dead in his kitchen, I was immediately intrigued by the presence of two isolated tins of dog food on his kitchen table.

There were no other groceries present - and plenty of cupboard space available in his substantial kitchen, making them conspicuous, to say the least...so why were they there?

We later found out that Peter Chapman would appear to have had recently returned from a dirty weekend in *Bathcombe Bay*. A stay maybe decided upon at the last minute...even on impulse, given that it would appear Deborah Knowles was not yet aware that she herself, was already out of the picture in the rapidly changing merry-go-round that was Peter Chapman's love life! and Peter's team-mates were largely unaware that he was unavailable for that Saturday's fixture.

So Peter Chapman desires the company of an attractive young lady for the weekend...he does not require the affections of his faithful *Yorkshire Terrier!*

The tins were therefore left in a convenient, and easy to spot, place for a hastily commissioned dog sitter. But who to look after the *Yorky* whilst he was away??

By all accounts, Peter Chapman did not have many friends left in this world of ours...impressionable young ladies aside! I believe that is why, once the eye had been deposited with you at *Police Headquarters*, your boys had such a late start in trying to identify its owner. No one was missing a loved one you see...no one would report him missing!'

'Yes - we had trouble even trying to find somebody to formally identify his body would you believe!'

'One thing he still did have though, was a brother - one Richard Chapman.

Richard Chapman was not from the area, but still kept in touch with his brother - and being surrounded locally by many an enemy and spurned lady (all of his own doing I might add), Richard was the only person Peter Chapman would - and could, trust with a key to his property. So Peter asked a favour of his sibling, and Richard duly obliged'

'Poor old Richard Chapman' added Kent.

'Yes, an unfortunate, and fatal, coincidence, that Richard Chapman agreeing to walk and feed his brother's dog...would coincide with our murderer executing a plan that they had been putting together for some time!'

'So what do you think transpired with respect to Richard Chapman then?'

'Ok. So early that Friday morning...and early enough that he can complete the promised chore before his own day's work began, I think he parks up at Peter Chapman's property, in the blue vehicle we found abandoned in *Folestree Parva*. He then lets himself into his brother's house, picks up the dog leash - and takes the *Yorky* for his morning walk.

It's a little chilly first thing in the morning, so he first grabs his brother's coat from the coat stand, locks the front door and heads down the drive, and into *Rowley Woods*.

Peter Chapman was wearing this same coat in the photograph we found and subsequently used for my article.

When not in use, this coat would be hung right next to the front door on the hat and coat stand...which is exactly where we found the pale green summer jacket, that Peter Chapman had worn whilst staying in *Bathcombe Bay* - and had hung there when he returned to his house.

I guess Peter Chapman had told his brother, many a time, where to walk the dog - but as a creature of habit, the *Yorky* was likely to lead him there anyway. And why not? - with a beauty spot literally on your doorstep, and extensive woodland pathways making an ideal playground for our four-legged friends.

Our murderer has been conducting discreet reconnaissance for quite some time. Who knows how many times they might have wandered up from the direction of the cricket club? - and right through *Rowley Woods* to the lay-by entrance near the driveway to Peter Chapman's barn conversion?'

'...From the cricket club??' exclaimed Kent (*he was animated*): 'Who?...who do you think is our murderer Davieson??'

The Welshman smiled. The Chief Inspector's tone was demanding, and he would keep this theory to himself no more:

'Alan Chambers Chief Inspector!'

Davieson stared Kent directly in the eye.

The Chief Inspector stared back - with his mouth gaping wide open. He was speechless.

'Alan Chambers??'

The Chief Inspector's brows furrowed...he looked sceptical.

'May I continue??'

'Yes - go on'

'Well, it proved an ideal spot to pry on his intended victim, and in due time he would know all Peter Chapman's regular movements - including when he walked his dog, where he walked his dog...and the route they would take.

So early that morning, Richard Chapman enters *Rowley Woods,* unaware he is being observed, and lets the dog off the leash. He places the leash in the pocket of his brother's coat, as the dog runs off to explore and play.

He is a man. He is a man arriving from Peter Chapman's driveway. He is a man arriving from Peter Chapman's driveway - walking Peter's Chapman's *Yorkshire Terrier*. He is a man arriving from Peter Chapman's driveway - walking Peter Chapman's *Yorkshire Terrier*...and wearing Peter Chapman's coat!'

'You don't have to labour the point Davieson!'
The journalist smiled:

'I think I do Chief Inspector. When Alan Chambers runs Richard Chapman through from behind, with Ted Ellis' three-pronged turf aerating fork...he cannot see his victim's face and he thought that he had murdered Peter Chapman!

The oversight was not helped by his rapidly-deteriorating eyesight...but more on that in a minute or two!

I would suggest, that this sickening act - or merely the fact that Richard Chapman is no longing keeping up with our four-legged friend, attracts the attention of the faithful *Yorkshire Terrier*. The dog then, understandably, returns to investigate. It is maybe aggressive...it is certainly a problem, and so it is dispatched in the same clinical and cold way as the dog's new walker has been.

He cannot risk leaving incriminating evidence at the murder scene in *Rowley Woods* and so Alan Chambers is prepared. He is wearing both Ted Ellis' gardening gloves - and his size eleven *Wellington* boots. No fingerprints to be left on any murder weapon - and no tell-tale footprints that might be traced back to himself either.

I know you have spent quite some time, Chief Inspector, in trying to identify possible suspects who take a size eleven shoe or boot!

What you had not considered, however, is that generally anyone with *slightly smaller* feet could always get away with wearing a larger shoe or boot. It is not nearly so easy to squeeze a larger foot into a smaller shoe - but unless the foot was tiny, most would manage without it bringing too much difficulty in walking around - without them slipping off...or appearing comedic or clown-like.

Anyway, it had always been Alan Chambers intention to bury the corpse of Peter Chapman in *Rowley Woods*, once he had killed him. That is why he took Ted Ellis' shovel when he made preparations for his plan.

In taking a proper look at the face of the man he has just murdered, however, he realises (to his horror I would suggest!) that it is not Peter Chapman he will be burying - but some entirely innocent, and unknown, individual who has somehow gotten himself involved in the morning's affairs.

Alan Chamber's original plan is off-piste.

He searches the pockets of the coat Richard Chapman is wearing (his brother Peter's coat of course) and finds Peter Chapman's house keys in one of the pockets - and Richard Chapman's car keys.

He, errr...pockets these, before he instead, buries the bodies of Richard Chapman, and Peter Chapman's *Yorkshire Terrier*. The dog is a tiny thing of course and can easily be dragged off a sufficient distance away from the first grave to prevent the need for an overly obvious pile of loose earth when burying the bodies. And that is why, Chief Inspector, no keys of any description were found on the person of Richard Chapman.

This had not been Alan Chambers plan, as I said - but *in for a penny...in for a pound*. He decides that he will go to Peter Chapman's house and confront him there.

The house is quiet, and there is no sign of Peter Chapman's expensive motor. He knocks on the door, but there is no answer. He tries the house keys in the front door - and it opens.

Alan Chambers enters Peter Chapman's house...and waits.

It is still Friday morning.

At this stage he has no idea, of course, that Peter Chapman is away at the coast - and will be until Sunday afternoon...but he is now past the point of no return, and must see this thing out in its entirety.

Over the course of that weekend, this sees him searching Peter Chapman's fridge and food cupboards, to keep his inevitable hunger at bay. He had not thought he would be there for two and a half days of course!

He gets by on simple cheese sandwiches and glasses of tap water. He may have lost his usual appetite, given what he had already done?? - I don't know...but it is enough.

Sometime late Sunday afternoon...maybe early evening - and having already said goodbye to Jodi Fletcher, Peter Chapman arrives home.

He sees his brother's blue car parked on his drive and parks his own car in the garage. He locks the garage, walks to the house - and unlocks his front door. He expects to find his brother, Richard, inside. Richard - maybe having checked in on his dog one last time, and maybe having thought that he would stay for a quick cuppa or beer, and a catch up, with his brother before heading off home.

Peter has no idea that in actual fact, his murderer is waiting for him inside, ready to take him by surprise, run him through with the aerating fork...and afterwards mutilate his body!

Out of the shadows - or maybe even complete darkness springs Alan Chambers, and the third victim is ruthlessly dispatched as the other two before him. Peter Chapman doesn't stand a chance, he likely suffers little...and Alan Chambers has finally got his man!

Peter Chapman's inability to answer his front door thereafter, would later frustrate Jodi Fletcher - who, you informed me, wanted to pick up with Peter where they had left off at *Bathcombe Bay* - and Deborah Knowles, who informed me herself that she too was missing Peter's company at the club, and had therefore decided to try and see him at his house when her husband Andrew slipped out of their own house and she had unobserved time to herself'

'It would go on to frustrate Andrew Knowles too' added Kent.

Davieson nodded:

'Anyway...back to the immediate scene of the crime:

Alan Chambers crudely removes Peter Chapman's eye and, extracts a tooth. This was his original plan back on some kind of course - and the reason he had taken Ted's screwdriver and pliers, amongst other items.

He vacates the house and locks the front door behind him with the spare set of house keys. He then lets himself into Richard Chapman's car and drives away from the second murder scene. I do not think that he ideally would have done such a thing - but desperate times call for desperate measures Chief Inspector!

This is the car he used to drive to *Folestree Parva* when he despatched the eye to Geoffrey Wright'

'Why Geoffrey Wright??' asked Kent.

'Well, he still held Geoffrey Wright *partially* responsible for Roger's accident, Chief Inspector. He felt Geoffrey Wright, as the umpire that day, never should have allowed himself to be bullied into letting play continue in such poor light.

Alan Chambers thought this was irresponsible, and that Geoffrey Wright should take some accountability for Roger's injuries...he decided then, to shake him up and at least frighten him!

The car is ultimately an inconvenience, *very* unfamiliar to drive - and not easy to explain away, so having safely removed it from Peter Chapman's property, and used it to begin his postal plans - he abandons it in *Folestree Parva*.

With his eyesight as poor as it is (I do promise to get onto that shortly), I daresay any parking signage would largely be lost on him anyway - and he may very well have parked up there illegally, without any realisation that he had done so!'

'How did he get back to the post office later on then, to post the tooth?'

'He used his bicycle Chief Inspector'

'His *bicycle??*'

'Yes, the postmaster eventually recalled that Alan Chambers had been a customer at the post office...and then left on a bicycle.

I had also noted that Alan Chambers no longer possessed a car. There was no car on his drive - and no garage to house a car in either. His driving licence had lapsed, and he was disqualified from driving due to his deteriorating eyesight.

This deterioration of the eyesight is also why he is no longer the scorer for *Upper Woodleigh Cricket Club!*'

'Your case for considering Alan Chambers is certainly compelling Davieson - but I must admit that once you had convinced me that there was a possibility of there being *Biblical inspiration* behind the murder (or at least mutilation)...I was convinced that Roger Lenton was our man'

'You were?'

'Yes. It seemed so obvious - *eye for an eye* and all that! He loses an eye and I could quite conceive him having let the dust settle for a couple of years - removing himself from the cricket club scene, planning all this in the interim...then picking his moment when Peter Chapman had least expected it'

'Ah - but then you said that Roger Lenton's Bible was *the cleanest thing in his house!* Chief Inspector'

'Did I??'

'You did'

'Well I was probably being sarcastic'

'Maybe...but I think not Chief Inspector. No, it reminded me of a sermon I heard in our chapel as a little boy in *South Wales*'

'It did??'

'Yes. There the Reverend stood one Sunday morning at *Morning Worship*, and he asked all the Sunday School children to come up to the front, and sit down in front of him. My mother duly sent me to the front of the church, with the other children'

Kent nodded politely. *He wasn't sure exactly where Davieson was going with this.*

'He then holds up two Bibles. The one in his left hand is in immaculate condition, pristine - and unspoilt. The other in his right, however, was tattered, and dog-eared.

He asks us *which of these two Bibles is the best??*

Of course, we all enthusiastically point to the first one - the pristine one.

He slowly shakes his head and informs us that the pristine Bible makes him feel a little sad, as it has obviously not been read and studied. Whereas the other one has clearly enjoyed being lovingly read and referred to. It was obviously well used.

Good sermon that!...pitched perfectly at the Sunday School children at the front - but contains something (indeed plenty) for all their parents, sat in the pews behind them.

Roger Lenton's Bible was clean because he rarely, if ever, used it. Alan Chambers' copy, on the other hand, was well-thumbed! In fact, when I took a sneaky peek at it, I found that it contained a bookmark lodged at precisely the passage of Scripture that *St. Catherine's Bible Study Class* had only just collectively read as part of their programme of theological discourse.

Alan is a member of the local *Bible Study Class* of course!'

The Chief Inspector listened intently, and started to silently nod his head faster and faster:

'Ok Davieson. You make such a compelling case, and the way you manage to present this so logically, so thoughtfully - and so eloquently...well, you make it all seem so straightforward!'

The Welshman beamed.

'In short Davieson - you've convinced me that we should get over to see Mr. Chambers sharpish!...'

Chapter Forty-Four

They were back at Alan Chamber's house - Davieson (it was his hunch after all) and a significant police presence headed by Kent.

There was no answer at the front door, so they tried the gate that led through to the back of the property. They passed his bicycle propped against the house and proceeded through to the back.

Then they found him!

He was hanging by his neck from a tree in his garden - all decked out in club tie and club blazer...he was a funny colour, and well beyond saving!

They noticed the patio doors, leading on to the garden at the back of the house, were open and the curtains inside were moving slowly in the gentle summer breeze.

With the Chief Inspector leading, they entered the house single file and stepped into Alan Chamber's kitchen.

They then found the note lying on the kitchen table.

There - absolutely in the centre of an otherwise empty kitchen table, was an envelope addressed to *Chief Inspector Kent* in the incredibly neat handwriting, Davieson recognised from the scorecard.

It was Davieson who had first coughed and nodded his head towards it.

Kent looked over at whatever the Welshman was indicating, strode across, put on his gloves - and opened the envelope...it had not been sealed. He removed an equally neat letter from inside it and laid it flat on the table so that both men could read it.

This they did in silence, whilst the others waited on at a distance, until Kent instructed them further:

I'm sure that many will deem what I have done, a peculiar form of justice for the modern age.

Others of a religious or moralistic persuasion may be uncomfortable with how all of this sits with the sixth commandment??

Well after that, Deuteronomy tells us in Chapter 19, verses 19-21, to put the evil away from amongst us - eye for eye, tooth for tooth.

Well, I have done that Chief Inspector. I put the evil away. Peter Chapman was evil and had near destroyed our family club. We were traditionally close-knit, best of friends - and couldn't do enough for each other.

Peter Chapman arrived on the scene - and in his own loathsome way, went about upsetting just about anyone he came into contact with. A bully, a womaniser, aggressive - an idiot, and a nasty piece of work!

Roger's accident may have been enough to break the camel's back - but he was still at it right up to the end of his days, divisive, abusing players - and even fisticuffs with one of them.

I largely kept out of his differences - but one can only sit around for so long and see your friends and colleagues destroyed by the man. Somebody had to do something about it and my blood had boiled for quite long enough!

Many of our club membership had been injured directly by the man...either physically, mentally - or both, and they risked putting themselves under immediate suspicion, had they attempted to do anything about this. Yes, most of them had plenty to look forward to - and the rest of their lives ahead of them.

I, on the other hand (and excusing the cricketing pun), consider that I have had a good innings. I could take the risk...I could take one for the team! I would not, Chief Inspector, want an innocent man or woman condemned if they were pushed into doing what I have done - so I was the only realistic option to remove this evil from our midst.

So ancient retribution it may well be - and I myself tossed and turned many a night over that sixth Commandment...which pre-dates the passage from Deuteronomy?

What will our Maker make of me? you may ask - for I have killed Chief Inspector! And killed one entirely innocent man in error too. I am truly sorry for ending the life of Richard Chapman, and any sorrow I have brought upon his friends and relations, as a result of this error.

I am sorry about the dog too. It was a spur of the moment thing as it ran back towards me that morning in the woods - having been let off the lead. It may have been aggressive - it was certainly yapping and noisy...I could neither risk being bitten - nor afford the attention it might bring until I had hidden what I had done. Ordinarily, I would never wish a creature harm of course.

Am I sorry about killing Peter Chapman??
NO, I AM NOT!

He probably did not suffer (a shame really) - in that I had turned off the kitchen light, lurking with intent patiently in the doorway- and took him completely by surprise.

God is the giver of life. He gives...and He takes away, says Job (Chapter 1, verse 21). Well, I am afraid that I am now ready to upset the Psalmist (Psalm 31, verse 15) and take my life into my own hands.

I ask that nobody makes a fuss at my passing, but hope that in my own way, I have allowed Upper Woodleigh Cricket Club to bring closure to this difficult and unsavoury period of our, otherwise illustrious, fine history...and move forward on a more pleasant and harmonious footing.

Alan Chambers

Chapter Forty-Five

Shortly after it had opened, Davieson parked up, headed in - and walked up to the counter area.

The Welshman ordered a coffee, and took a seat in the window bay, at table number five.

The cafe in *Lower Woodleigh* was largely empty and nice and quiet. It was just as he had remembered it from a previous visit, and why he had specifically chosen it over possibly more populous alternatives.

Kent had informed him that the police were comfortable that there were no suspicious circumstances - and that Alan Chambers had indeed taken his own life.

Ted Ellis' missing working tools and boots had eventually turned up in the vicinity of *Folestree Parva* after *Haverton Borough Council* responded to a fly-tipping complaint.

According to Kent, the tines on Ted's fork were still razor-sharp - and being driven three times through differing sets of rib cages had not appeared to blunt them in the slightest!

They had evidently proven too cumbersome for Alan Chambers to dispose of on his bicycle, and so he had offloaded them whilst he still had use of Richard Chapman's car, and on his trip out to the post office there.

Kent also informed him that he had finally agreed to release the body of Peter Chapman for cremation. They neither of them thought the cremation service would be anything other than derisory in attendance!

He unfolded his copy of *The Morning Chronicle*, placed it neatly on the table in front of him, and patiently awaited the delivery of his order before turning the page.

He gazed down at the front page through oval-shaped spectacles. A photo inset showed the official police photograph they had taken of Alan Chambers' *King James Bible*.

The Evil From Among You! ran the accompanying headline...

THE END

Acknowledgements

I would like to express my gratitude to my two beta readers: Andy Buck - and my Mother, Maureen Gregory.

I would also like to thank Robin Dearden - an excellent photographer and a good friend. It is a photograph of myself that Robin took on one of our many walking holidays together in the beautiful Lake District, that I use in my author branding and marketing materials.

About The Author

Paul Francis Gregory is a long-time fan of classic detective fiction, and would much rather read, and try to unravel himself, those whodunits of the golden-age - than something overly-modern, hard boiled and deeply forensic.

This love of the genre (in particular the canon of Agatha Christie and Conan Doyle) has inspired the almost timeless setting within his work.

As well as reading and writing, the author enjoys watching his beloved Leicester City Football Club - 4 times FA Cup Runners-up...eventual Premier League Champions, Fell Walking in the Lake District and Running/Racing.

Paul lives in North West Leicestershire, is married to Dawn - and has 1 daughter and 2 step-sons.

https://www.amazon.co.uk/-/e/B01N4LYL4V

https://pfgregory.wordpress.com/

https://www.facebook.com/Kindly-Invited-To-Murder-a-novel-by-PF-Gregory-1837097583236305/?ref=aymt_homepage_panel

By The Same Author

Kindly Invited To Murder

Your wedding day is meant to be one of the happiest days of your life.

Susannah and Stephen Hall's wedding day started ok, but then there was a fatality and their joy was short-lived.

Merv Davieson is chief crime reporter at *The Morning Chronicle*. Could his journalistic approach get to the bottom of the matter, whilst the official police investigation stalls and fails?

Printed in Poland
by Amazon Fulfillment
Poland Sp. z o.o., Wrocław